BROTAN THE BREEDER

Brotan the Breeder

DAEL FOREST

NEW ENGLISH LIBRARY
TIMES MIRROR

A New English Library Original Publication

*

FIRST NEL PAPERBACK EDITION JUNE 1975

*

NEL Books are published by
New English Library Limited from Barnard's Inn, Holborn, London, E.C.1.
Made and printed in Great Britain by Hunt Barnard Printing Ltd., Aylesbury, Bucks.

45002311 7

CHAPTER ONE

As dawn dispelled the darkness of night the guards at Rome's gates barred the entrance of bullock wagons and carts; they wouldn't be allowed in again until nightfall. Already the city's narrow, flag-stoned streets were filling with slaves bound on errands, litter-bearers carrying their masters to business, freedmen engaged on personal missions and clients paying courtesy calls upon their patrons. Rome awoke swiftly, the daylight hours too precious to squander. Traders set up stalls, shopkeepers displayed their wares and customers' chairs were set outside barbers' shops. Soon the thoroughfares were so thronged all needed to shout and push to make headway.

Rome awoke and its citizens pursued their many ways of life. The coppersmith's hammers rang, bakers and pastry-cooks stoked their furnaces, while in the households of the wealthy, slaves busily swept and scrubbed.

A new day dawned for everyone and as Hadrian the architect's handmaiden kneeled before him he could not resist the impulse to stoop and kiss her softly upon the nape of her neck. For long her pride and her resentment of slavery had thwarted him. But time had matured Haesel and when she looked up, the tenderness in her eyes aroused Hadrian's passion. But he had much to do and knowing it Haesel quickly looked down again and adjusted the folds of his toga. Hadrian was building a new city and before noon he must interview many clients and seal many contracts. Despite the great need they shared for each other, she had to remain his slave until they had planned their future life.

Many streets away another woman who had given Hadrian great happiness sat before her mirror while her maid applied cosmetics to her pale cheeks. Since the chariot crash which had caused Juno's death, Una had been numb with grief. He'd died in her arms and something inside Una had died with him. Marcus, the young surgeon who had attended Juno, had called often to comfort her and with patience and persistence, had persuaded her to accompany him to the park. Now, as mascara was spread upon Una's eyelashes, she felt a stirring of interest at the thought of going out after so long behind four walls. Was she beginning to live again, she wondered?

At that moment Melanos, who despite her grace and beauty delighted in competing with men in their manly sports, proudly caressed her swollen belly. 'I compete with men,' she told her handmaidens complacently. 'But men cannot compete with us women. *This,* they could *never* achieve!' The girls laughed as they washed her with perfumed water and brushed her hair.

'And you, Mertice,' teased Melanos, who had increasingly confined herself to home and the companionship of her more intimate slaves as her pregnancy progressed: 'Will you care for my babe, when I hunt with the men again and prove myself their better with bow and arrow?'

'Oh, I will,' breathed Mertice. Her eyes shone.

Melanos eyed her shrewdly. 'You would wish for your own child if you were not a slave?'

Mertice flushed. 'It is not to be thought of, Mistress.'

'Have you recovered from your silly infatuation for that ridiculous Alexander?'

'I think of him differently now,' admitted Mertice. She flushed even more as she thought of the sensitive hands of Steward Octavius who understood so well a woman's emotions.

'Do you not despise Alexander?' asked Melanos wonderingly.

'I am not sure, Mistress.'

'He stripped you of dignity, had your head shorn and made

of you a humiliating public spectacle. Yet *still* you do not hate him?'

'I do not know, Mistress.'

'Then you must meet him again and learn what is truly in your heart and mind.'

'Yes, Mistress.'

Melanos's eyes gleamed mischievously. 'We will make fine game with Alexander,' she promised. 'If it is your wish, girl, we will find a way for you to take revenge.'

'Yes, Mistress,' whispered Mertice.

At that moment, Mertice's brother Redwald was selling a block of stocks and shares at a price which would gain him and his Master a satisfying profit. Although a slave, his shrewd trading enabled him to earn much more than most freedmen. His brother Thane, far from Rome and a slave working to help build the city that Hadrian had designed, had not found financial fortune. But he had learned that his strong hands, guided by an unexpected talent, could sculpture stone into beauty. The fulfilment he found in this work made him richer than most men.

There was a third brother, Saelig. His pantomime had won him the admiration of all Rome. As Toros, his miming filled the theatre and his frenziedly applauding audiences were loath to have him leave the stage. But Saelig did not wish his miming art to become a harassing labour and intended to leave the theatre. This morning he was mounting his horse at his villa in Baiae to ride into Rome. Areta heard the hoof-beats as he cantered past her villa and stepped out on to the terrace to blow him a kiss. Saelig saw her and turned in his saddle to give her a sweeping bow.

Diocles was proud of the appetite that kept him chubby and good-humoured. Unlike most Romans he breakfasted leisurely and greedily. He believed that man should pursue *all* physical pleasures, and Diocles practised what he preached. He relaxed on his reclining couch and feasted his eyes upon the delicacies piled high upon the table, and upon the nudity of his serving-girls. They had been chosen for their youth and their beauty. Some fed him, placing choice morsels upon his tongue, delicately wiped his lips with napkins, then held a goblet of sweet wine to his lips for him to sip. Others bathed his chubby body with perfumed water while one well-practised in the art, kneeled beside him and teasingly provoked his male desire with sensitive fingers. Behind him a lovely slave plucked the string of a harp and sang to delight his ear.

But when his wife Valle joined him, Diocles knew she was disturbed. She rarely left her bedchamber so early. He gulped the crushed almonds a slave popped into his mouth, licked her fingers clean, teased her nipples until she giggled and then asked bluntly, 'What ails you, Valle?'

She had come straight from her bed with her hair dishevelled. Her face was startlingly white without make-up, and betrayed her age. 'I am worried about Poppea,' she said.

Diocles' interest quickened. Poppea was young, vivacious and a radiant beauty. He delighted in sharing a reclining couch with Poppea at feasts. Surprisingly, she had a genuine affection for Diocles despite the difference in their years and his flabby, over-indulged flesh. Her friendship was valuable to him because Poppea's husband was influential at Court and Poppea's persuasiveness gained Diocles many business favours.

'What troubles Poppea?' he asked.

'She has gone mad!' burst out Valle. 'She throws discretion to the winds, is wildly reckless and will bring disaster upon herself if she is not brought to her senses.' She paused and added meaningly. 'And upon her friends!'

Valle's consternation alarmed Diocles. He rested his fingers gently upon the head of the girl who kneeled beside him, signalled her delicate fingers to desist from their subtle stimulation. He willed his pleasure-befuddled mind to think clearly. 'Explain yourself, woman.'

'Poppea has a male slave escort named Strabo. He is big; but alongside Poppea he looks a giant. He is a magnificent animal, but dull-witted.'

'And so?' demanded Diocles, impatiently. He was exasperated by the new fashion trend. Society women sought impressive male slaves to use as escorts. They squandered hours planning how to robe them, competing against other rich women to create the most sensational spectacle.

'It happened on the night of *Bona Dea*.' said Valle. 'That should have warned me because Poppea suggested it; and she was High Priestess.'

Diocles grunted. *Bona Dea* was part of the worship of Isis, the Goddess of fertility, practiced only by women. There was sincere reverence in the ritual, which inflamed the passions of the worshippers until they were demented by sexual lust. It culminated in a frenzied orgy. Social protocol was abandoned for the night, the doors of the worshipping chamber were flung open, and any passing male was seized upon to satiate the passions of women who'd lashed themselves into a frenzy of desire. Grist could always be found to grind between the writhing thighs of the worshippers; household slaves, litter-bearers and freedmen – even nobles enticed in from the streets. A smile of reminiscence touched Diocles' lips as he recalled being pounced upon by naked, desire-demented women, their loins and breasts wet with the wine and potions that had inflamed their senses, who'd dragged him to the worship chamber to be stripped and cherished.

'*Bona Dea* was an excuse Poppea used to have her way with Strabo,' said Valle.

'It is condoned,' stated Diocles. 'A mistress may have her way with any and every slave on the night of *Bona Dea*. It shows true reverence for Isis, our beloved Goddess,' he added piously.

'But Poppea has lost her senses,' wailed Valle. 'She has tasted fruits that have bewitched her. Her hunger cannot be appeased. The scandal is known to servants of all households. Poppea is possessed and cannot leave Strabo alone. She rarely ventures abroad and at all other times Strabo is in her bed-chamber. He arouses strange lusts within her she cannot satisfy. Her desires are so strong she indulges them recklessly and dementedly. She no longer tries to keep them secret. If she does not come to her senses soon, all Rome will know of her madness!'

Diocles frowned. This was serious. A mistress who debased herself with a slave became an object of ridicule and was laughed out of society. Litirus would then be bound to put aside his wife to safeguard his dignity. That would be serious for Diocles. If Poppea could not practice her persuasive wiles upon her husband, he would lose a valuable business contact. 'I will think about it,' he growled.

'You must *do* something,' urged Valle. She felt genuine concern for Poppea, who was her friend.

Diocles pointed to a pastry stuffed with minced chicken-liver and anchovy and as it was raised to his lips, signalled the butterfly fingers to resume their delicious teasing. He closed his eyes, concentrated, and recalled Strabo. Poppea's escort, he remembered, had diverted them at a feast when Strabo had demonstrated his male virility with an outdoor slave. The girl had been a virgin and it had been entertaining. But a costly entertainment, Diocles remembered. The girl had become pregnat and he'd leased her out for three years to avoid the resultant problems. A bad business when slaves were so costly. He put the slave from his mind and pondered the problem of Strabo.

He didn't even remember that the virgin slave's name was Fabia.

CHAPTER TWO

Fabia was apprehensive. She'd been brought from Diocles' household and locked up in an outhouse with many others. The age of her companion slaves ranged from fourteen to thirty. All were newly pregnant. As the days passed, more pregnant slaves joined them and now there were thirty-five altogether. They had learned that today they would leave this place and travel far from Rome to a new household where they would work, bear their children and labour until three years had elapsed. Then they would return to their masters, if they were still wanted. Fabia was sixteen and had been born into slavery. She was owned and must always obey. She dreaded her future but was resigned to it.

At dawn rice and bread was served and when the slaves had eaten their fill, stewards ordered them out into the patio where they stood in line. There were two bullock carts, one loaded with provisions for a long journey and one stacked high with bales of wool. Six lance-bearing soldiers who had been hired to protect the caravan waited by the courtyard gates. There were also four household guards, one a husky youth no more than fourteen years of age.

A rope was attached to the back of a cart and the first girl was ordered out of line. The rope was looped around her neck and tied so that it would not draw tight and choke her. Around the walls of the patio stood great bales of raw wool. Stewards brought a bale to the first slave and fastened it upon her. The load was supported by a bamboo frame that rested upon the slave's back and head. Her load towered high. A second slave was ordered from line, the rope was looped around her neck and she too was laden with a towering burden of raw wool.

When is was Fabia's turn she stepped forward submissively. The rope was greasy with use and limp around her throat. Two stewards warned her to brace herself, lifted up her load and placed it upon her. Her head bore most of the weight and there was padding where the bamboo frame rested upon her spine. Ropes to hold it in position were drawn tight around her waist, over her shoulders and under her armpits. Fabia was strong and accustomed to labour and her load seemed bearable. But by the time the last slave had been roped in line the weight bearing down upon her had become tiring.

All was ready. The young guard climbed up on to the first wagon, shouted and lashed the bullocks. The cart jolted out through the courtyard gates followed by the second cart. Behind, in single file like beads threaded on a string, followed the thirty-five pregnant slaves, stumbling uncertainly as they adjusted their gait to their towering loads which threatened to tumble them off balance. At the rear followed the soldiers and household guards.

The caravan moved with painful slowness through the crowded streets. Market traders often refused to move their stalls until the soldiers intervened. Citizens mocked the slaves, who hung their heads like beasts of burden. Sometimes youths grabbed at them intimately, laughing uproariously when the slaves' natural defensive movements almost made them overbalance. This angered the guards. One youth who snatched at Fabia's breast was caught, beaten, kicked and left huddled in dust and blood.

There was an argument with sentries at the city gates because it was forbidden for carts to leave the city by day. But a soldier produced a permit, the barriers were lowered and the caravan began its long journey.

The bullocks' pace was ponderous but as the hours passed

Fabia found the temptation to rest almost irresistible. The sun beat down remorselessly and her ankle length chiton stuck to her, sweat-stained, upon her breasts and belly. But she was grateful for it's protection from the chafe of the ropes under her armpits. Her load became almost intolerable, bearing down upon her head and shoulders until her feet were leaden. But she struggled on. One girl had fallen and the guards had whipped her legs until blood stained her chiton. Fabia did not want to suffer that. She learned that short, shuffling steps made it easier to balance her load and she watched the rope that linked her to the girl in front so that it never pulled taut. She stumbled on in a stupor, her mind drugged by the heat and the weight that crushed her down, blind to all except the heels of the girl who trudged before her and deaf to all but her own laboured breathing. The dust stirred up by many dragging feet caked upon her sweat-wet brow and cheeks, encrusted her eyelashes, clogged her nostrils and parched her throat.

When the caravan halted Fabia thought it was the end of a long day. But they had been on the road only six hours. This was the mid-day break. The girls were ordered to sit, and then lowered themselves gingerly. The halt was too brief to remove their burdens but the relief of easing their legs was great. The household guards passed along the line of slaves with wet cloths to wipe their faces clean of dust, and with water flagons from which each girl drank her fill. Then came bowls of rice mingled with crumbled bread and dried figs. The food was plentiful, but like Fabia, most of the girls had little appetite. There was glorious relaxation while the soldiers and the guards sat at a distance from the slaves and ate their own meal. Their leather wine flagons passed many times from hand to hand, but all too soon they were ready to move on again and ordered the girls to their feet. Almost all had to be assisted to stand up by the guards and soldiers, and it was misery to force their aching bodies into movement again. But when the sun passed its zenith and dropped towards the horizon the girls regained strength. Their tired muscles had adapted to the rhythm of the slow walking pace, and the stupor that gripped them lessened. They became more aware of their surroundings and the good-natured joking of the guards and soldiers who walked beside them. It was ribald jesting, much of it coarse and lewd flattery. A soldier fell into step beside Fabia, walking with an unhampered, upright ease she envied. His bronze helmet gleamed in the sun and the overlapping metal-plated strips of leather that overhung his short kilt clinked musically in rhythm with his stride. 'Stand up straight, girl,' he teased. 'Don't hunch like an old crone.' And when she did not answer he added encouragingly 'Soon you will grow accustomed to your burden. Then you will skip and dance as though it does not weigh you down.'

'I have only a woman's strength,' she panted. The weight upon her head did not permit her to turn her face to his.

'You are young and healthy,' he chuckled. 'You could carry ten times your burden with ease.' His coarse fingers squeezed her breasts, then slid down to her thigh, pinching to test its plumpness. 'You'll serve well,' he said. But he'd noticed how she'd shrunk from his touch and added warningly. 'Sticks can break bones.' He left her then and walked beside the girl in front. He talked to her while his hands moved upon her, not carressingly, but like a farmer judging livestock.

It was dusk before the caravan halted again. Soldiers and guards passed along the line of slaves, removing their burdens from their shoulders. When the crushing weight was removed from Fabia she sank to the ground with enormous relief. Guards and soldiers brought the exhausted girls bowls of water, allowing them to wash. The slaves were accustomed to going bare-footed but so much walking had caused cuts and blisters which the guards washed and bandaged solicitously. There was still a great distance for the slaves to walk. Then bowls of rice, bread and dried figs circulated, the slaves ate and drank their fill, and then were left to take their ease as they could, remaining strung together, and with the hard ground for their mattress. But the girls were so weary they could have slept anywhere.

The men tethered the bullocks, lit a fire and roasted meat. The wine flagons circulated and laughter betrayed the men's high spirits as they gorged themselves. Fabia swiftly fell asleep but awoke with a start. The camp-fire had died but she saw the shadowy figure of a soldier stooping over the girl alongside her. The soldier kneeled and then his shadow merged with the slave's.

Fabia drove her nails into the palms of her hands and shivered with dread because she was a slave and must always submit. She tried to shut her ears to the soft human sounds and the awful menace of man.

The night held the sound of many men's voices, their coarse laughter mingling with the high-pitched protests of girls.

Presently, the shadow beside her split apart as the soldier arose to his feet. He disappeared into the night and Fabia breathed again, knowing there were thirty-five slaves but only six soldiers and four guards. If she was lucky she might not draw their attention. It was this reassuring thought that enabled her to sleep.

CHAPTER THREE

Guards awakened the girls before dawn with cuffs and kicks, fed them and fastened their loads upon their backs. But today the burdens were not so unbearably heavy and they were impatient with the slow plodding of the bullocks which made their journey longer. There was little fear the rope that linked the slaves might become taut. On the contrary, they had to use care not to tread on each other's heels. They even noticed the countryside. It was parched scrubland with stony and infertile hills in the distance. Coarse sun-yellowed grass grew between rocks and only occasional stunted trees miraculously drew moisture from the dry soil. Frequently, the caravan had to circle around impenetrable clumps of cactus. The sky was blue and the sun blazed down.

Fabia's hair was greasy and damp with sweat, her chiton stuck to her and perspiration trickled down her legs. She raised her garment as she walked, tore strips from its hem and used them to ease the chafing bite of the ropes around her armpits. She'd adapted to the rhythm of ceaseless walking and after the midday break was able to gain her feet without assistance. Later, a household guard walked beside her. By swivelling her eyes sideways she saw he was no more than twenty and with curling black hair that fell to his shoulders. He was sun-bronzed and his eyes a startling blue. His short tunic, fastened on his right shoulder, left his breast bared. His ornamental belt carrying a scabbard and short stabbing sword showed he was a trusted slave with the rank of Overseer.

'Does your burden grow easier?' he asked and she was surprised at the gentleness of his voice, for he was one of the guards who had whipped the girl who had fallen.

'It is bearable,' she panted. She wiped sweat from her brow and cheeks.

'The first days are hard. But each day is more bearable.'

'How many days must we travel thus?'

'Seven. Perhaps eight.'

'Our destination is far from Rome?' she asked.

He chuckled. 'For those who walk. But two days riding on a fast horse.'

'I doubt I have the strength to walk so far.'

'Nonsense. You household slaves have lived too softly. Labour will strengthen your back and loins. A pregnant woman needs preparation for the birth.'

'What will happen to me?' she asked bleakly.

'You will bear a strong and healthy son,' he encouraged. 'Afterwards, you will do a woman's work. It will not be unpleasant. What is your name?'

'My name is Fabia.'

'Listen, Fabia. Tonight I will come to you.'

She froze. Something inside her cringed and he was aware of it. For some paces he was silent. Then he asked: 'How did you come to be with child?'

'It was my Master's wish. He ordered me from my sleeping quarters when he was feasting with his guests. There was a male slave. A giant!' Fabia's voice faltered. 'It was my Master's wish,' she added.

He paced beside her. 'And you were a *virgin*?'

'I was not aware what would happen.' She shuddered. 'I cried out and the guests laughed. So this male slave sought to entertain them with my pain.'

'You are not the first,' he said wisely. 'Nor will you be the last.'

She thought he had taken pity upon her but then he said: 'I will come to you tonight.'

She lowered her head and despair throbbed within her. But she was a slave and her body must yield to the wishes of her masters. Stoically, she resigned herself to what must come.

The long day reached its close, the caravan halted and the exhausted girls sank to the ground. Fabia had previously eaten little but tonight she was ravenous. When the bowl of rice and bread was before her she plunged both hands into it, scooped up food and crammed it into her mouth. She signalled for the bowl many times before her hunger was appeased. It was only then, as she scraped a hollow in the ground for her hip when she settled down to sleep that her fear of the night sharpened. She lay awake, listening to the men around the campfire, wishing their feasting would never cease. A slave should never think of escape, but for one wild moment she thought of sawing through the rope that linked her to the other slaves with a sharp stone and vanishing into the night. But that was madness. She could only wander, lost and afraid, and when found would be severely punished. She must brace herself to endure what man would inflict upon her.

All too soon the flames of the campfire died and the men around it melted away. The gruff voices of guards mingled with women's and soon a shadowy figure appeared, stooped momentarily over the girl alongside Fabia, moved on and loomed over her. She lay completely passive, her arms limp at her sides, but her hands tightly clenched. He lowered himself beside her, not quite touching her. But she shuddered at his nearness. He propped himself up on one arm and she could see the shadowy smile upon his face. 'I have kept my promise, Fabia. I have come to you.'

She turned her head away from him and lay motionless. He chuckled. He moved. He made of her chiton a tight roll across her throat and under her armpits. She shivered uncontrollably, but not with the cold of the night air upon her flesh. She kept her face averted and braced herself.

Yet, when it happened, it was not what she had feared. His hand upon her breast was as gentle as thistle-down. It moved caressingly and its touch was bearable; quite, quite different from what she had known. The caressing was so soothing that she relaxed, until with alarm she knew deeply disturbing emotions. Startled, she turned to look wonderingly into his face. The whites of his eyes glowed as he smiled and nodded. 'Do not fear, Fabia. This is how it should have been.'

She looked down upon herself and saw the darkness of his hand gliding downwards over the faintly glowing whiteness of her belly and gasped at the sharpness of new and unexpected sensations. Her head swam and she closed her eyes, confused and bemused. Where was the brutal thrusting and rending she had dreaded? Now there was no hint of pain, only a quickly mounting excitement that thrilled through her, tingled deliciously, swept her up and overwhelmed her until her senses whirled madly in a tidal wave of sweetness. She clung to him fiercely, unaware that her nails gouged deeply into his flesh, sobbing and whimpering while the tidal wave slowly subsided until she could relax again, her breasts heaving. She was grateful his hand was still upon her. And as if he understood her desires he propped himself up on one arm and smiled down into her face. 'You did not know it could be like this, Fabia?'

'It was never like this. I did not know what was happening. I was so greatly moved I almost lost myself.'

His hand moved again. Once more mysterious and delicious sensations stirred within her. She moved towards him instinctively, clasping him, eager for the pressure of his chest against her breasts. All of her responded abandonedly to his caressing and when she pulled him down upon her, loins writhed with their eagerness to receive him. She drove her nails into his back and gasped and huffed against his cheek until the whirlwind released her to drift down softly to earth.

'That was how it should have been, Fabia,' he said softly.

His hard, muscular weight was comforting and she tightened her arms around him when he moved. 'Do not go.'

'It is time. You must rest and gain strength for tomorrow.'

'What is your name?'

'I am Serbo.'

'You have made me very happy, Serbo.'

He chuckled. 'I have pleased myself.' He pulled away. But she twined her limbs around him.

'Do not leave me, Serbo.'

'It is time,' he said gruffly. He untwined her arms from around his neck and pulled away forcefully. 'You will sleep well,' he said and laughed as he arose to his feet.

For a long time she lay as he had left her, as though still relishing the joy of his flesh against hers. Then she pulled down her chiton and with a pleased smile composed herself to sleep. Her thoughts were of Serbo. He lived with her in her dreams and he was still with her when she woke in the morning.

CHAPTER FOUR

All day, as the caravan laboured onwards, Fabia thought about Serbo with the memory a pleasing pressure between her thighs. Her eye constantly sought him and her heart beat more quickly when she glimpsed him. She was sad he did not fall into step beside her and talk to her. But that night Fabia watched the men feasting around the campfire with impatience, instead of dread. When she saw a shadow looming up out of the darkness she closed her eyes and smiled expectantly. But it was a soldier and in the first moment of realisation she resisted until he slapped her face. She lay passively then, filled with an ache of misery. But he was not unkind, and although less patient than Serbo, was not unbearable. She did not wish it, but presently she clung to him as ardently as she had to Serbo; and he left her marvelling she could be so deeply moved. A little later, when another soldier awakened her, she received him meekly. After that there were soldiers and guards every night and in her mind they all strangely blended into Serbo. Once, when Serbo was near, she called to him. 'You did not come to me again,' she said.

She saw he only vaguely remembered her but when he said gruffly: 'It will be tonight,' she was content.

The caravan entered a mountainous region, threaded through valleys and spiralled around hills on paths that overhung precipitous drops. The steeply inclined and stony tracks were a severe trial upon the slaves but they had grown inured to their burdens and walked surefootedly. It was dangerous country offering good cover for brigands who lay in ambush. But the guards drew their swords whenever the caravan penetrated thickly wooded valleys and six soldiers and four guards were a formidable force. The caravan descended to the plains on the side of the mountain range without molestation.

They camped for the last time on the eighth night when already within sight of their destination. At dawn the slaves could see upon a distant hilltop a grey stone building, surrounded by high walls set amid acres of cultivated fields. But because they walked in single file behind the wagons, three or four hours elapsed before they saw the building again. By then the walls towered high above them and extended either side as far as their eyes could reach. Massive doors opened, the caravan passed through into a vast courtyard, guards shouted orders and the column of slaves was led to a storehouse. They stacked their loads of wool in a storehouse and unloaded the bullock wagons before they were allowed to rest. They were weary but relieved the journey was over. They joked and flirted with the soldiers until the guards rapped orders. Then they were led across the courtyard to a massive wooden door which Serbo hammered upon many times before a sliding panel opened and eyes inspected him. Then bolts slid back, the door swung open and Serbo gestured the slaves to file inside. The door was bolted shut behind them.

They found themselves in a high-walled patio. Two young guards removed the rope halter that linked them together and teased them about their travel-bedraggled appearance, unkempt hair and dirtiness. The noose-knots were too tight for fingers to unravel but the guards loosened them with iron spikes. They stood the slaves in line, ordered them to remove their chitons and gathered up the clothing. Then they led them to a stone-lined pool fed by mountain spring-water gushing through an earthenware pipe. The water was ice-cold and breast-high. The slaves shivered as they scrubbed themselves, eager to sluice away the sweat and travel-dust. The guards supervised their washing. All had to immerse themselves completely. Any slave afraid to put her head under water was ordered to the side where guards grasped her and pushed her under. The cold ate into the slaves' flesh and bones until their skin tingled and turned mauve. They wailed miserably, their teeth chattered and they were numbed to feeling before the guards permitted them to leave the pool and dry in the hot sun. The guards went into a stone outbuilding while the slaves combed their wet hair with their fingers and rubbed life back into their numbed limbs. Presently, a guard came to the door of the building and called a name. The slave stepped forward and he beckoned her inside. Soon, he reappeared and called another name.

When Fabia was called she was apprehensive. But the guard was friendly and reassuringly took her arm, led her to a stool in the centre of the chamber and sat her down. He picked up a sheaf of papyrus forms and consulted one. 'You are Fabia?'

'Yes.'

'To which household are you enslaved?'

'My master is Diocles.'

The guard confirmed it from the papyrus. 'That is correct.'

Another guard selected a leather collar from many which lay upon a bench. All had numbers burnt into them and all bore a metal ring to which a rope could be attached. 'She will be number 212,' he said.

The first guard noted the number on Fabia's papyrus record. Fabia shrunk away when the guard approached her with the collar but he chuckled. 'Do not fear. There will be no pain.' He lifted up her damp hair and fitted the collar around her neck. 'Is it loose enough, girl?'

'Yes,' she whispered.

He marked the overlap of the collar with his thumbnail, took it to a bench and pierced holes in it. He placed it around Fabia's neck again and passed soft iron rivets through the holes. 'Do not be afraid. There will be no pain.' He showed her how she must hold her head. But she shuddered at the sight of an iron instrument resembling long tongs. The tongs were gently eased between the collar and her neck and both guards united their strength and flattened the heads of the rivets. 'There! It didn't hurt at all, did it?' chuckled the guard. 'Is it comfortable?'

Fabia raised tentative fingers to her collar. It was greasy with use and fitted loosely. Soon she would grow used to it and forget she wore it. She fingered the rivets deeply embedded in the leather and knew she could never remove the collar without aid.

'Remember your number,' ordered the guard. 'Two One Two. Always answer to it.' He drew her to her feet, led her to another door, slapped her affectionately and pushed her through it. 'You're a comely girl,' he said approvingly. 'You'll serve well.'

Fabia and the other slaves waited like livestock in a cattle market until the last girl was collared. Then they were led out into the sunlight, across the courtyard and into another patio. Bowls of water and food were brought and after some hours they were led back across the courtyard and into a large chamber with a long low wooden bench in its centre. There was a wooden writing table against the wall. They waited. 'What work must we do?' one girl asked a guard.

'Patience,' said the guard. 'First you must see a surgeon.'

The surgeon was a man of thirty with the earnest face of a dedicated man. He wore a white linen tunic with a gold-thread embroidered hem. His clerk's tunic was of simpler design. The clerk sat at the table and set out his record books and colamus writing instruments.

Surgeon Malem sent a slow glance travelling over the naked slaves and saw there were no obviously unhealthy girls among them. He grunted approval. At his insistence pregnant slaves were now properly examined in Rome and the undesirable ones rejected. He pointed to the nearest girl and then at the low bench. The slave understood and lay upon it. He moved her hair to one side to see her collar. 'Number eight two,' he said. His clerk repeated the number and then entered it in the records. The surgeon frowned at the rope-burns that wealed the slave's armpits and waist, and applied a soothing ointment. As he worked he questioned the girl, nodding at her answers and making comments for his clerk to note down. 'Breasts normal,' he said. His sensitive fingers probed her belly, and then the slave obediently drew up her knees and parted them. Presently the surgeon straightened up and said: 'Probably thirteen weeks. It could be fourteen.'

'Thirteen or fourteen weeks,' repeated the clerk.

'Maternity,' said Surgeon Malem.

A guard stepped forward with a strip of red linen which he tied to the slave's collar ring.

'Next,' snapped the Surgeon and a second slave took the place of the first.

All the girls were examined and classified for maternity. Then the guards herded them along corridors and through a door into what at first seemed a world peopled by children and pregnant women. The girls gazed around in wonderment, slowly absorbing all they saw.

They had entered a vast courtyard surrounded by high walls. The sides of the courtyard were roofed in but the centre was open to the sky. One wall was lined with straw on which the women slept at night, and another wall was occupied by long lines of wickerwork cots. Another section was devoted to cooking, and big, blackened pots simmered over charcoal fires. Another section was the Infirmary where maternity beds were fitted with footboards and straining ropes. There were many more infants than women and the air rang with their squeals as they played in the sun. Motherly women supervised their games and scolded the naughty.

An Overseer faced the girls, a woman of forty with an air of authority. She wore a sackcloth tunic with a rope girdle from which hung a whip. 'Listen carefully,' she instructed. 'You are classified as maternity. Never remove the red tag from your collar. You will address me as Mistress. Until your labour, you will work within this compound. At first, you will perform the heavier tasks. But as your time approaches your work will be taken over by new arrivals. You will sweep and clean, care for babies that need attention, cook and serve. You must not attempt to leave this compound. I will allocate your work and you will obey only *my* orders. I am here at all times if you wish to speak to me. The life isn't hard and you should be happy. But disobedience is punished in many ways. Do you wish to ask questions?'

There were no questions.

Fabia was set to work in the kitchen.

CHAPTER FIVE

Brotan the Breeder was proud of his title. He'd been twenty-five years of age and a trusted slave when his wealthy master had promised him his freedom at the age of thirty if he could take over the Farm and make it profitable. Brotan had accepted the challenge, left Rome, and devoted himself to breeding.

After a few day's study he knew the Farm could not even cover its costs without drastic changes. Slaves bred slowly and had to be fed until the age of fourteen. Although they laboured in the fields when children, they consumed all they produced. Brotan saw that slave breeding could only be profitable if combined with industrial production. For days he pondered upon the problem, devised schemes and moulded them to suit his plans. He thought logically, and finally knew how to make the Farm profitable. But it was a Herculean task. He had only a run-down Farm and incompetent staff to work with. But with unflagging vigour, by uprooting and discarding what was useless, and building anew despite the cost, he succeeded.

He foresaw it was essential to have his stockyard divided into separate compounds where breeding and production could be combined. So every man, woman and child who could be spared from farming he set to building a high wall around the farmhouse enclosing two acres of land. Inner walls divided this rectangle into vast courtyards, all easily accessible to the others.

The courtyards were partially roofed in on all sides to give shelter to those confined within them.

Brotan had an inspired plan to provide himself with breeding stock. Pregnant household slaves were a bugbear to their Roman masters. Brotan contracted to care for these slaves through their pregnacy, keep their offspring and return the slaves to their masters after three years. A contract clause permitted him to buy the slave at the end of three years if he wished, at an agreed price. His offer was eagerly accepted and now there was never a shortage of pregnant slaves flowing into his Farm.

The largest courtyard he converted into a weaving factory. In the fields around the farm he grew flax. Its fibres were spun into thread and woven into cloth within the factory. When tributes of raw wool were sent to Rome he bought if the price was right, and turned it into good quality cloth.

Brotan's industry was rewarding. At the end of five years he was granted his freedom. But Brotan was a dedicated man who believed he had only merely begun to put the Farm upon its feet. He accepted his freedom but asked to continue his stewardship of the Farm.

That had been twenty years ago and Brotan still enjoyed his stewardship and constantly devised new ways to streamline production. There had been great changes in those twenty years. The old farmhouse had been pulled down and replaced by a magnificent three-storey residence and offices. Brotan's luxurious living quarters were on the top floor. From the terrace where he was now relaxed, he could look out over all the courtyards and see most of what went on within them.

As Brotan reclined on his couch, sipping sweet wine, he mentally reviewed his production system. He had an intake of about thirty pregnant slaves a month. They produced about three hundred and fifty baby slaves a year. Slaves sold for high prices these days and this annual production yielded a high profit. But after giving birth the young mothers could be 'sent to the guards' and inseminated again. A good breeder could deliver three children for Brotan before her contract expired. Those who did not conceive again were transferred to the worksheds and devoted two years of labour to weaving and spinning. The less nimble-fingered girls laboured in the fields, or were used for building. There were always a hundred and fifty women in various stages of pregnancy who cared for the children. At the age of five the infants were transferred to another courtyard and, supervised by pregnant women, spent their days spinning fibre into thread. At the age of ten the girls were transferred to the factory courtyard where they continued spinning and learned weaving. The boys were transferred to workshops to break down raw flax into fibre and comb wool in readiness for spinning. It was well co-ordinated, reflected Brotan with satisfaction. The slaves were utilised to the maximum and the combination of breeding and industry yielded large profits. With the passing of the years, even the problem of finding satisfactory males had been solved. With an average of one hundred and fifty males reaching maturity every year, stud guards could be selected from among them. There were twenty guards; young and vigorous men of magnificent physique, hand-chosen for their powerful virility. It was routine for them to serve one, two or more times daily. They were contented men who lived well, their duties light. They supervised, marched slaves to the fields to labour and patrolled the courtyards, tingling the legs of slaves who slacked with the tip of a whip. The guards' quarters was a large airy chamber with every convenience for their leisure hours. Three slaves cooked their meals, served them, washed their linen and kept their chamber cool and clean. Their palliasses of good quality sackcloth were frequently re-stuffed with fresh straw and were always sweet-smelling. There was direct access from the maternity compound to the guards' chamber. This facilitated the fertilising of nursing mothers who had to leave the guards' chamber at intervals to feed their babes. A week was usually long enough to fertilise a female. Brotan liked statistics. Twenty lusty guards with a vigorous sexual drive could serve forty to sixty times daily. Since there were rarely more than twenty females at a time sent to the guards for fertilising, the probability of their swift conception was high. Indeed, the birth rate would have been very high but for the recognised infertility of Roman females. A disturbing decline in the birth-rate had been noticed since the turn of the century. Many women were barren, many miscarried and few had more than two children. Among household slaves too, good breeders were rare. So whenever Brotan had the good fortune to receive one, he took advantage of the contract clause and bought her.

He looked up and smiled a welcome when Surgeon Malem entered and sank down on a reclining couch opposite him. A slave brought wine and fruit and bathed the surgeon's brow, arms and legs with scented water while the two men talked.

Brotan was delighted with the young surgeon. Five years ago, when the old surgeon who had served the Farm all his life retired, Brotan had had misgivings about this younger and less experienced man. But Malem had quickly proved he was a better surgeon, and had brought a new dimension to breeding. Surgeon Malem's revolutionary ideas, seemingly reckless and costly, had proved invaluable in practice. The two had quarrelled bitterly at first. Brotan's policy was to shave costs to the bone and work slaves to the maximum. It was only to allow the young surgeon to see for himself how mistaken he was, that Brotan eventually approved his recommendations. Under Malem's schemes, instead of factory slaves working from the time they awoke until they fell asleep on their legs, with only a brief midday break to gulp down food, they were given a long midday break, rest and recreation before bed, and occasional rest days when they did not work at all! At frightening expense the slaves had been allowed all the food they could eat, its quality and variety was improved and some slaves had been appointed to squander valuable labour upon cooking. Even limited quantities of meat, fish and fruit had been recklessly wasted on slaves.

But the mad theory worked! The emaciated, spiritless factory slaves had filled out and gained vigour. They now laughed and talked while they worked, despite which their production was much higher even though they worked shorter hours. They were more resistant to illness and the mortality rate had declined startlingly. There were also other striking improvements. Childbirth deaths dropped, the rate of conception increased, and the special medical attention Malem demanded for newborn babies yielded remarkable results. The young surgeon insisted upon individual cots, napkins and warm coverings. Even specially prepared weaning foods! He established regular feeding intervals and insisted upon frequent washing. When Brotan saw that almost all of Malem's babies survived through the first two difficult years, he realised the old surgeon, who'd lost more than half his charges before their second year, was an incompetent old fool.

Malem had other theories Brotan encouraged. The young surgeon had a mania for records. He insisted good breeding was a matter of administration. He studied his records to learn how to make females prolific, knew which mothers produced the healthiest off-spring, and sought to learn the reason for it. He was so dedicated to his work he often irritated Brotan with his preoccupation with trivialities. He irritated Brotan now. Brotan had asked conversationally: 'How was the new batch today?'

Malem frowned. 'They were fit.' He eyed Brotan meaningly. 'My *insistence* upon a medical examination in Rome, and rejection of the unhealthy, was well advised!'

Brotan had not wanted the expense of medical examinations. But he had to agree that slaves who collapsed on the journey were a nuisance. 'It was a good suggestion,' he admitted reluctantly.

But Malem was merely preparing the ground for his next request. 'Good leather straps must be substituted for rope,' he insisted. 'All suffered varying degrees of rope burns. Some were severe.'

'You said they are healthy,' defended Brotan. 'They'll heal.'

'Wide straps,' insisted Malem.

'Slaves expect to suffer a little pain,' evaded Brotan.

'You misunderstand,' said Malem. 'Frequently; armpit weals do not heal. They ulcerate and fill with puss. If they do not heal before their labour, it spoils the quality of their milk. The infants suffer!'

'It is too costly,' wailed Brotan. Leather was expensive and Brotan instinctively cut costs. He'd frequently crossed swords with Malem about costs. There was only one economy upon which Malem agreed with him fully. The slaves went naked, and were issued sackcloth smocks only during the cold months. At the first hint of spring warmness the smocks were collected and stored until the following winter. In this way the smocks lasted many years. But Malem had only agreed with him because he believed open air and sunshine kept the slaves healthy. 'Leather is costly!' wailed Brotan.

'With broader straps they can carry a few pounds more,' persuaded Malem artfully.

'It shall be done then,' sighed Brotan. He comforted himself with the thought that slave porterage *did* save wool transport costs.

'Twins were born today,' mentioned Malem with satisfaction.

'Will they live?'

'They're fine and healthy.' Malem's brow furrowed. 'If I can learn why some females bear twins we could double output.'

'Perhaps it is the male,' suggested Brotan vaguely.

Malem sighed. 'Twins are so rare. The few records I possess give no hint of the cause. We've only had eleven cases in five years. Seven were new intakes. Four were fertilised by our guards. One was a negress whose children were black, and the other three were Caucasian females.'

A slave brought bowls of food, placed them on the table between the two men, then kneeled beside Brotan, ready to feed him the delicacies he indicated. If he had wished, a slave would have served Malem. But he had a strange impatience with leisurely living.

'The caravan returns to Rome tomorrow,' mentioned Brotan. 'Forty-two expired contracts. They'll carry a good load. It's a big delivery of cloth to the Emperor's garrison; a new clothing issue to his army.'

'But straps must be fitted to the load-frames before the next batch leaves Rome,' Malem insisted.

Brotan sighed. 'It shall be done,' he promised. 'I shall also send twenty of our slaves to be auctioned. Did you prepare a list?'

Some children matured earlier than others. Some were physically developed at the age of fourteen while others needed one or two years more before they could be classed as adults. It was Malem who decided when a slave was ripe and likely to bring the highest price. 'There's seven males and thirteen females,' he told Brotan. 'One female is defective. An accident at birth. One leg slightly shorter than the other. She walks with a limp but is strong, can work hard and is worthy of a good price.'

'Is she comely?'

'Her form is pleasing. She has a pleasant smile.'

'Men would find her attractive?'

'I believe so.'

'Then she can be sold to a susceptor who will value her more than a work slave.' Brotan chuckled. 'If she is attractive, men will be bemused and her short leg will not be noticed when she is lying down.'

Malem had eaten sparingly. Now he arose. 'There is a slave in labour now,' he excused himself. 'I must attend her.'

'Take your ease,' advised Brotan. 'You drive yourself unnecessarily. There are women to help.'

'This slave has narrow hips and a small pelvis,' said Surgeon Malem. 'I don't wish to lose the child.' He hurried away.

Brotan motioned the serving slave to sit beside him and caress him. He was disappointed that Malem had hurried away. The surgeon was so obsessed with his work the two men had little opportunity to converse. Brotan would have liked to have known Malem better, not as a surgeon, but as a person. He knew little about the young man's private life and thoughts. Indeed, Brotan often felt lonely and would have enjoyed companionable conversation with another man.

What did Malem do for sexual gratification? Brotan wondered. He'd never discovered and was curious. Brotan usually visited the factory and strolled around until his interest was kindled. He chose the youngest and comeliest. But only those with a strip of black linen tied to their neck collar. It indicated they were infertile. If the girl was pleasing he kept her in his quarters while he had the whim. Some had proved themselves good serving girls and he'd retained them. Not infrequently he had five or six slaves simultaneously serving him and pleasing his senses. It was the only extravagance with slave labour he permitted.

But Malem, who spent his life among the slaves could indulge himself at will. He could even break the household rule and take a slave due for the slave market. Perhaps that comely girl with the short leg? But such slaves should leave the factory as virgins; and during Malem's service there had been no complaints from dissatisfied clients. Did Malem then choose green-tagged slaves who were to be fertilised? Or did he, like Brotan, choose only the infertile?

Brotan would have liked to have known.

Brotan himself always chose with great care. It would have troubled him to know the vigour of his loins had bred his child into slavery. He wanted to know if Malem had the same qualms.

CHAPTER SIX

Although a night birth had cost Malem his sleep he began his rounds at the usual hour. His clerk knew from the records which slaves should be examined that day and an overseer had them lined up and waiting. But Malem first visited the new mothers who were lying on palliasses. The slave with narrow hips was pale. She'd had a difficult labour and had lost blood. Malem prescribed a strong meat soup to help her regain strength. The mother of twins was weak but recovering swiftly. Malem passed on to the line of waiting slaves who'd recently borne children. The first had green eyes which jogged his memory about her. She was firmly fleshed and had promise of being a good breeder. Only three weeks had elapsed since she'd given birth but already she was very fit and her flesh healed.

'How old?' Malem asked.

'Fourteen, Sire,' answered the Overseer.

Malem nodded his satisfaction. The younger they bred the better they adapted to breeding. Three weeks was early to begin her fertilisation again, but she was fit for it. 'Two weeks with the guards,' he ordered. Then with a rare attempt at humour added; 'Green for green eyes.' The Overseer removed the red tag from the slave's collar and replaced it with a green tag.

The next three young mothers were still not well enough for fertilisation. The clerk noted that they were to be examined again in a week. The next slave was the Farm's finest breeder. Malem had fourteen stock breeders of whom the youngest was twenty-two and had borne seven children. The slave before Malem now was thirty-eight and had borne eighteen children. She was a comely slave with shapely limbs, clear eyes and a serene face. She would have looked younger than her years except for her breasts and belly. Her breasts hung low like shrunken skin pouches. But now she was suckling again they had rounded out with milk around the nipples. Her belly had been so often stretched to its maximum it had lost its natural elasticity and the wrinkled flesh hung in deep, limp folds. This slave had been given collar Number One as a token of honour, and Malem believed she might bear a total of twenty . . . or even more! All her children were strong and healthy and two sons had grown up to be chosen as guards. Childbearing was now effortless for this slave and a week's repose was all she needed. 'Give her a Green,' Malem ordered. 'One week with the guards.'

The slave looked at the Overseer and for a moment the two women seemed to commune silently.

'*Two* weeks with the guards,' said the Overseer as she changed the collar tag.

'One week,' corrected Malem.

The Overseer understood and sympathised with the slaves' problems, and often fought minor battles for them. 'Can it not be two weeks, Sire?' she asked.

'A week is enough. She conceives like a rabbit. One day would probably be sufficient.'

'A concession to the slave, Sire. Only one week with the guards is little consolation for many months of carrying.'

Malem scowled. He liked to keep the numbers of females being served by the guards at a minimum. Frequency and variety of service rendered best results. 'Slaves are here to breed, not to be consoled,' he reprimanded the Overseer. Then he relented and added gruffly: 'I'll decide next week.'

Almost two months had elapsed since the next slave had spent two weeks with the guards. Malem always tried to diagnose pregnancy at the earliest moment. He examined her digitally, hoping the hardening of her womb might be noticeable. It wasn't. He sighed with disappointment and told his clerk he would examine her again in a week's time. The next three slaves were eleven weeks from the guards chamber and he easily confirmed that they were pregnant. Their green tag was changed to the red maternity tag. All three slaves were still suckling their previous child.

The next slave was seven months pregnant, with her second child. When she'd conceived her milk had been abundant and rich but Malem had a theory. He squeezed one breast gently until a bead of milk hung from the nipple. He took the bead between finger and thumb and tested it for texture and stickiness. He squeezed the breast again, coaxing milk on to his palm. He tasted the sample delicately, his brow furrowed. 'Definitely inadequate,' he said and his clerk recorded it. 'It's watery.'

Malem had suspected that the milk of nursing mothers who became pregnant lost its quality. When the growing embryo in the womb made new demands upon the mother, her suckling suffered. Now he'd proved it to his satisfaction. New-born babies needed good nourishment until they grew strong. But not all mothers give good milk. Some yielded rich milk in abundance while others gave little and of poor quality. Malem had weeded out his best milk-givers and today made his weekly check of them. There were more than a dozen feeders, most of whom had suckled non-stop for more than two years. Their nature had adapted to the rhythm of non-stop feeding. They were provided a special diet of nourishing food and were forbidden to exert themselves. Malem had also trained them in breast care, scrupulously washing and drying their nipples after feeding and when he examined them he was delighted there was no soreness and that even his gentle handling proved milk to flow easily. All feeders bore red tags, warning they were not to be fertilised. Malem intended to keep them suckling as long as possible. For many years he hoped. They would only be fertilised when their milk dried up.

The next four slaves had been sent to the guards after giving birth, had not conceived and had been sent to the guards a second time. Three months had to elapse now before he could be sure if they had conceived. None were good breeders and in the meantime, their labour could be utilised. He ordered brown tags for them. This meant they were to be transferred to factory, or farm, labour until their next examination.

Malem then passed along the rows of baby cots, eyeing the infants with satisfaction. They were well cared for. There was an abundance of red-tag slaves who were filled with maternal love which they gave freely to all babies because few mothers ever learned which was their own baby. All newly-born babes were nourished only by the wet-nurses whose rich milk made them grow strong. Mothers weak from childbirth, and those with inferior milk, suckled only the older infants. Malem encouraged breast feeding as long as possible and babes were weaned only when there was a lack of milk to nourish the older babies. He insisted upon regularity in feeding and a crude time-piece signalled feeding times. A wooden see-saw held down by a heavy weight balanced a large copper bowl into which water dripped from a tank. When the bowl filled, its weight tipped up the see-saw and this signalled feeding time.

Malem strolled around the vast courtyard, eyeing the playing children and the slaves who cared for them, and occasionally examining a child or a slave. He moved on to the kitchen, inspected pots and utensils and tasted the food being prepared. He noticed that the straw the slaves slept upon was wet and smelly and ordered it to be changed. Then the Overseer unbolted a door and followed him into the child compound.

At the age of five all children were transferred to this compound for five years. At the age of ten the girls were transferred to work with adult females and the boys were transferred to undergo special training. In this compound the infants slept, ate and played, as well as worked. Red-tag slaves cooked and cared for them, and an Overseer supervised their labour. The children sat cross-legged in columns. Under one arm they held a hank of flax-fibre which they fed to the spinning-wheel they held in their other hand, twisting fibre into thread. The older children were dexterous. Their spindles shimmered, spinning in the sun, and thread seemed to grow from their nimble fingers. Even five-year olds achieved some success, winding lumpy thread on to their spindles. Three children with suspected illnesses were awaiting Malem. He treated them and then inspected the living quarters. The slave who cooked for them was in the seventh month of pregnancy. She moved slowly, favouring her distended belly. Malem frowned at the Overseer. 'Why is she transferred here from maternity?'

'It is only for a few days, Sire.' The Overseer was embarrassed.

'There is a reason?'

'She has three children here and likes to be near them, Sire.'

Malem scowled. Few children knew or remembered their mothers, who left the Farm when their contracts expired. It irked him that routine should be subjected to sentimentality. But good breeders were rare, this slave had produced eleven offspring and he reluctantly granted her a privilege. 'Two days more,' he said gruffly. 'Then back to maternity.'

He visited the weaving factory. The great courtyard seethed with industry. The young females spun wool and flax into thread, while the older ones stretched, treated and dyed the yarn. Hundreds of iron pegs hammered into the ground with long threads stretched from them in parallel lines formed crude weaving frames. As nimble fingers inter-wove other threads between them a skilled overseer ensured the weaving was well finished. There was coarsely woven sackcloth, finer sackcloth for tunics, and soft and heavy cloth woven from wool which would be made into togas and pallas.

The Clerk's records showed which slaves Malem was due to examine. His probing fingers soon learnt that three were pregnant. They were red-tagged and sent to maternity. Many others he ordered to the guards for another attempt at fertilisation. The last slave made him ponder. She'd been sent to the guards twice without conceiving. But she had the sturdy hips of a good breeder, and he was loathe to give her a black infertility tag. 'Try this one again for a week,' he ordered. 'Each day to be served by six guards; and by ten on her last day.'

The last two slaves brought to him had reached the age of thirteen. Their breasts were formed and their female characteristics developed. In a year they'd be ripe for the slave market.

He ordered them to be given a numbered collar in place of their leather anklets, and to be trained to serve as household slaves.

Malem still had much to do, but it was noon and he was hungry. He hurried away to join Brotan who was already reclining at the food-laden table.

CHAPTER SEVEN

Brotan had been busy checking the caravan he was despatching to Rome. The biggest bullock wagon was so laden with cloth it groaned under the weight. The other was loaded with food; rice and stale bread for the contract-expired slaves in whom Brotan had no more interest, a fattening and substantial diet for the slaves he was sending for auction, and meat and fruits for the soldiers and guards who had the responsibility of delivering the caravan safely to Rome. Brotan watched the caravan set off, two soldiers leading the way, a bullock wagon rolling ponderously behind them, and a long column of slaves staggering under their loads of woven cloth. One stumbled and fell, pulling down the slave behind her and Brotan nodded approval when guards whipped their legs soundly before dragging them to their feet. Behind the load-bearers marched two more soldiers at the head of the thirteen female slaves who were to be sold. They wore new, sackcloth smocks. Two more soldiers separated them away from the young males who also wore sackcloth tunics. Household guards brought up the rear of the caravan.

'If my orders are disobeyed, your head will pay for it,' Brotan warned his head guard.

The man protested that he could be trusted.

'No female is to be touched,' repeated Brotan. 'Contract slaves must be returned to their masters unfertilised.'

'That is what we *all* understand, Sire,' protested the guard.

'The Farm's slaves are virgin. They must remain thus!'

'They will, Sire.'

'You must guard them against the young male slaves. Hot blood is uncontrollable. They must be kept away from the females and watched closely.'

'It will be done, Sire.'

'The female who limps. If she cannot be auctioned get a good price for her from a brothel.'

'You must trust me, Sire.'

'Also leather straps,' grumbled Brotan. 'The bamboo frames must be fitted with broad straps.'

'I will attend to it, Sire. It will make our journey back easier. The slaves will complain less.'

Brotan dismissed him. 'On your way then!'

Brotan had then inspected his domain. He'd whisked swiftly through maternity, confident that Surgeon Malem could be trusted implicitly, but loitered in the weaving compound, inspecting the finished material and tongue-lashing overseers for shoddy work. Then he'd paced up and down the fibre-preparing compound, growling at the overseers who in turn used their whips until work speeded up to its maximum. Preparing flax and wool fibre for spinning was undertaken only by male slaves over ten. The wool was washed thoroughly many times, combed into strands and then carded. Flax was crushed and then slit open to release the inner fibres. Despite his display of dissatisfaction however, Brotan lingered in the all-male compound. Most of the time he was deluged by females, females and females. It was a pleasing contrast to be with young men who worked quietly and efficiently, instead of twittering incessantly like magpies. He took pride in the boys as they grew strong and healthy. He had produced them and took a fatherly interest in them. He even felt a twinge of regret when youths he had seen grow to maturity were sent to the slave market. Not all were sold. Selected youths of fourteen were kept back to supervise the younger ones. At nineteen, if the promise they'd shown held good, they were promoted to the position of guard. Therefore, their sexual precocity was encouraged and the overseers reported it. There were now two thirteen-year olds who had all the makings of virile guards. An infertile female slave cooked and cleaned for the compound, and in rest periods shared the straw with these two adolescents. Brotan chuckled at her weary, harassed appearance and took pride that his young protegés had sapped her energy.

Brotan rode out then on horseback to inspect the great acreage of flax, corn, rice and vegetables that provided the Farm with food, and the raw material for the factory. He reined in his horse at a rice field and walked it to a guard who relaxed in the shade of an olive tree. The man rose to his feet respectfully when his Master approached.

'All is well?' asked Brotan.

'All is well, Sire.' The guard gestured towards a line of slaves knee-deep in water and linked together by a rope passed through their collar rings. They were stooped over with their backs to Brotan, uprooting rice seedlings for transplanting to a prepared rice field. Brotan was vaguely irritated by the sight. 'Stand them up,' he ordered.

The slaves straightened up, glanced over their shoulders curiously and then looked away quickly when they recognised their Master. They had dull eyes and peasant faces. Only slaves fit for nothing else laboured in the fields. 'It goes well?' Brotan asked.

'This field will be finished today, Sire. Tomorrow we transplant to the next field. Afterwards, they trim the parasite roots in the olive groves.'

When Brotan rode off the guard ordered the slaves to resume work. He relaxed in the shade, plucked a grass stalk to chew and studied the stooped-over slaves boredly. This week of duty rota in the fields was disagreeable. He preferred factory duty when, after a stroll around the compound, he could return to the guards' room and play dice. He noticed that one clumsy slave uprooted less seedlings than the others. He toyed with his whip lazily. In a while he'd speed her up, he decided.

Brotan finished his inspection of the fields and rode back to watch the slaves building a new wall. He was always expanding the Farm. He needed another compound for dyeing and tinting.

Rome was growing rapidly and consuming all he could supply. The wall was built of small stones cemented with a powdered volcanic rock. Neck-linked slaves balancing straw panniers on their heads bore the stones from the quarry to other slaves who mixed them with cement and poured them between wooden boards. Brotan was a Roman and he built soundly. The walls were a metre in width.

A guard came to meet Brotan and held his mount's bridle. 'All is well?' asked Brotan, his sharp eyes noticing the slaves' red weals.

'All is well, Sire,' said the guard, who prided himself on being easy going. But this morning the slaves had disagreed among themselves, dropped their panniers and fought each other. He'd been obliged to leave his cool shade and lash them apart, the exertion making him sweat.

Brotan watched a column of slaves reach a mound of stones and one by one heave the contents of their panniers on to the heap. Their bodies glistened with sweat, mingled with blood. Conscious of their Master's eye, they returned to the quarry and refilled their panniers with unusual haste.

'Tingle their flesh,' approved Brotan. 'Keep them working.' He kicked his mount's flanks, wheeled around and rode back to his quarters where his midday meal was awaiting him.

Malem joined him wearing his customary preoccupied frown and even before he began to eat said firmly. 'I must have an assistant.'

Brotan's mouth fell open. 'You have one!'

Malem gestured irritably. 'An unimaginative clerk, good only to keep records. I need another with medical knowledge, who can examine with confidence.'

'Extra cost!' grumbled Brotan.

Malem's eyes gleamed. 'Which will be earned many times over. The clerk must devote all his time to keeping records. We must know which slaves each guard has served, when, and how often.'

'Is it not enough that they serve them?'

'No!' Malem shook his head vigorously. 'There is a reason why some slaves bear twins. There must be reasons why other slaves do not conceive. Carefully kept records may show me these reasons.'

Brotan had a great respect for the surgeon's initiative. 'If it is necessary it shall be as you wish,' he conceded. For no good reason he suddenly remembered the line of slaves in the rice fields, stooped over as they dug in the mud for seedlings. At the same moment his slave wiped a crumb from his chin with a napkin. He knocked her hand away. 'These slaves are . . . animals!' he grumbled.

Malem looked at him curiously. 'We are all animals,' he said mildly.

'They're like . . . cows!' said Brotan. He didn't understand the annoyance he felt. 'They're docile . . . oafish . . . so ready to serve!'

'It is their destiny to serve. They are slaves.'

'They . . . *obey*!' complained Brotan. 'They are . . . *passive*! Does it ever anger you? Do you not feel the need of something . . . different?'

Malem chuckled. 'You long for the independence and arrogance of the free-born.'

'Perhaps,' grumbled Brotan. 'And you do not?'

Malem's eyes glowed. 'When I have the mood I take an infertile slave whose contract is about to expire. I assure her she will not be punished for disobeying a Master, and offer to give her freedom if she successfully resists me.' He pulled open his tunic to show his scratched shoulders and chest. 'They resist because they long for freedom, and because it is their instinct to resist.' He chuckled. 'I am strong and they never succeed.'

Brotan's blood ran hot as he visualised such a struggle and the final conquest. Malem was a man of ingenuity. But his curiosity was also aroused. 'Why choose infertile slaves?'

Malem thought the reason was obvious. 'Those whose contracts are expiring have laboured long without being serviced by the guards. Desire gnaws hotly within them and makes their final surrender very sweet.'

'Ah!' said Brotan and scowled. He felt this wasn't the moment to ask Malem if he would father a slave.

CHAPTER EIGHT

The slaves sent to the guards' chamber to be serviced sat cross-legged in the section allotted to them. They had straw beneath them and the wall to brace their shoulders against. While they waited they plaited rush mats. Here they were to remain for the number of days decreed by Surgeon Malem, leaving only if they were nursing mothers called away to give a feeding. The guards' own serving slaves brought them bowls of food and water when they were not busy attending to the guards' needs.

There were eleven slaves, and the green-eyed girl whose wide hips made Malem judge her to be a potential breeder was the first in line. Her name was Bala and as she plaited she brooded upon the quirk of fate that had brought her to this place. Bala had been an outdoor slave who had fallen in love with a handsome, golden-haired slave. They broke the household rules recklessly, and devised ways to spend forbidden hours together. The strength of their love overwhelmed caution and common sense, and when her condition was recognised she'd confessed. They'd both been brought before their master. But the golden-haired youth saved his own skin and accused Bala of tempting him until he yielded. She loved the youth and accepted all the blame. He was punished lightly, whereas she was whipped soundly and imprisoned without food or drink. The pain of her weals bore no comparison with the pain of her heart, which she suffered during her journey to the Farm. But later, as she swept, cleaned and tended the kitchen fire she grieved less and less for the youth as new life grew within her. When she was set to care for the babies she found happiness in their chortles and baby antics. She poured out love upon the young ones, hugging them to her swollen breasts and watching her belly distend with an anticipatory smile. When her time came it was easy, as though she was made for child-bearing. She rested two days. By then, her babe had been taken and nourished by the wet-nurses and nobody knew which was her child. The white numbered tags around all babies' wrists were meaningful only to Surgeon Malem's clerk. But her abundance of love she lavished upon all the babes she suckled. Her milk was rich and she was filled with joy by their tiny fingers and hungry mouths. She realised presently she had never been so happy. She had quite forgotten the golden-haired youth and had no wish to return to her master. When Surgeon Malem ordered a green tag to be attached to her collar, she was content. She plaited patiently, hurried away to feed the babies when it was time, and returned contentedly to await the guards' pleasure. There were many guards. They took supervisory strolls around the compounds and then returned to play dice, eat and drink, or scold and jest with the slaves who waited upon them. Bala was the first in line. When a guard approached and pointed to her she complacently put away her plaiting and followed him to his palliasse. Afterwards she took her place at the end of the line.

The farm's prize breeder, slave Number One, begrudged the time she spent feeding. But her sagging breasts were soon emptied and she hurried back to the guards' room with her loins aching with a hunger she felt could never be satiated. She was pleased there were many guards and only a few slaves to be served. While she waited she thought about her many children; so many it was difficult to recall them. She was breast-feeding the youngest, and three others were toddling. There were five in the children's compound, but she couldn't remember if it was three boys or three girls. Four more were with the adults; but it was so many years since she had seen them she didn't know if she would recognise them. Of the remaining eleven, nine had been auctioned in Rome and two had been promoted to be guards, to her pride.

She was first in line again and a guard was pointing. She rose to her feet and followed him eagerly. All the guards knew her well and jested with her affectionately. He lay beside her and buried his hand in the slack, doughy mound of tired flesh that was her belly, and pulled it up tent-shaped. 'We'll soon fill this out again,' he joked. Later, when the guards came in from the fields she was first in line again, and the one who beckoned her was one of her sons. He never acknowledged her and was more formal than the other guards. She did not question him about himself because it made him angry. But afterwards, when she took her place at the end of the line, she wondered if it was his seed that would fertilise her. But she knew she would never know because there were so many guards.

The slave Malem had been reluctant to classify as infertile, concentrated upon her plaiting and shut her mind to the present. She yearned to be returned to her owner. Only then would she live again. She'd entered his household at twelve and had trained to be his serving-girl. He was mature, wise and kind and she'd learned to anticipate his wishes. As she'd ripened into womanhood his gaze had rested upon her more often with admiration and affection. She'd stolen secretly to his bed-chamber at night and slipped away before dawn. His affection and love had won her completely. She would have died for him. When the Overseer had reported to him she'd conceived, she'd understood when her master had sent her away from his household without even a private word to her. He knew what was best. His wife would have been outraged by the truth and would have separated them for ever. But by bearing three years of separation patiently, she could return to his household and resume her place close to her master. She bore her child happily because it was her master's. But she was terrified of bearing another. The sagging breasts and loose-skinned bellies of the breeders filled her with horror. She dreaded returning to her master with her young beauty marred by child-bearing. She shuddered at the sight of the feeders, their enlarged nipples dripping milk at a touch. Her own milk was abundant and fearing being made a feeder, she *willed* her milk to stop flowing. Her strength of mind worked. Her milk dried up. She used all the strength of her *will* again when she was sent to the guards to be fertilised. And while they used her body she defied them, mentally closed her womb to their invasion and instead thought of her master and the joy of returning to him as lovely as when he had first loved her. She had not conceived and had been sent to work in the weaving factory. The second time she was sent to the guards she again resisted with her *will*, and again triumphed. She still did not conceive. She should have been black-tagged as infertile and left in peace to work out her contract. But Surgeon Malem, contrary to practice, had sent her to the guards a third time. And this time the guards had received special orders. They called upon her often and out of turn. She resisted with her *will*, but they were persistent and steadily wore her down. She steeled her womb to remain sealed while they invaded her body; but they bruised and pinched her flesh until she pretended to respond. They were skilful too and had ways to make her burn with a desire she tried to kill. Her *will* was strong. But they were too many. Her resistance steadily weakened until she was too weary to resist longer. Then the waves of aggression consumed her until she surrendered. Tears were hot upon her cheeks. She thought of her beloved master and feared she would never see him again. She choked with horror. She would become a breeder. She moaned piteously; but the guard with her twisted the soft flesh of her breasts until she responded as he wished.

After a long day of sweeping and cleaning Fabia sank down wearily upon her bed of straw. She had talked to other slaves and knew all there was to know about life in maternity. The slave who lay beside her asked: 'Do you miss the pleasure with the soldiers?'

'They made the journey less unpleasant,' admitted Fabia.

'It's the last pleasure you'll have for a long time,' said the slave and sighed. 'That's how it is here; a little pleasure and months paying for it. I've had two. My third's on the way. It's always the same; a few days with the guards and then months of waiting. I'm unlucky. I conceive easily. A week with the guards is all I need. They'll buy me and I'll become a breeder.'

'You can't be sure,' Fabia sympathised. 'You might never conceive again.'

The woman snorted. 'With these guards! You'd have to be barren!' She spat into the straw. 'The best is if you get a black tag, work out your contract and return to Rome.'

'There's nothing I can do about it,' wailed Fabia.

'Perhaps you can,' said the woman mysteriously. She lowered her voice. 'It can't help me now. But you're young. It might work.'

Fabia moved closer to the woman who whispered: 'There's a slave who came up with you who says she knows how to stop it happening. Talk to her tomorrow.'

It was a comforting thought. But Fabia dreamed of Serbo who strangely blended into many other guards and soldiers. And she smiled softly as she dreamed.

CHAPTER NINE

Brotan's caravan reached Rome after a seven day march. Denied the pleasure of dallying with the female slaves, the guards and soldiers were anxious to reach Rome and kept the caravan moving long after dusk.

Redwald, who had an astonishing flair for nosing out good business, galloped out and met the caravan when it was still five miles from the city. He bargained briskly, bought all the woven cloth not already promised, and paid cash for it. He galloped back to Rome with the bill of sale and samples of the consignment. Before the caravan reached the city gates he had re-sold the merchandise for a pleasing profit. It was bought by an agent who was loading one of Diocles' trading ships and had room for more cargo. The ship was bound for Barcino* where the natives loved to parade in colourful clothes and would barter for it with gold.

Brotan's contract-slaves were taken to the depot where they unloaded their burdens, and Marcus, the young surgeon, dressed their rope-burns. Then they were locked up until their Master's guards came to return them to their households.

The market-slaves were taken to Barba the Slaver who had a trading arrangement with Brotan. Barba inspected the merchandise and his experienced eye instantly picked out the slave

*Barcelona

with a short leg. He gestured her on one side. She waited with downcast eyes, feet together to conceal that one heel was a finger's thickness off the floor.

'This one is worthless!' growled Barba.

'She is comely,' protested the head guard.

Barba placed his finger under the girl's chin and lifted her face to his. 'Comeliness does not conceal a limp.'

'It is but a slight defect. She walks with ease.'

'Walk!' Barba ordered. The slave walked with one heel not quite touching the ground. But concealing the impediment gave her an unnatural gait. 'She limps!' said Barba flatly.

'She is young and strong. She can labour many years.'

'So can many who do not limp. Who will buy a *lame* slave!'

'She will cost less,' argued the head guard.

'*Much* less,' agreed Barba.

'How much less?'

'Take her away,' said Barba. 'Find a buyer of small means who is not proud of his household. My clients are wealthy. They seek virtues in their slaves, not deformities.'

The Head Guard tied a rope to the slave's collar and led her through the streets to the bawdy district frequented by drunken revellers. Here the narrow alleys were thronged with coarse labourers who sought cheap pleasures in crowded inns and taverns where wine was served hot to inflame the senses, where dice and knuckle-bones rattled, and gambling quarrels often erupted into bloody violence. The head guard pushed his way into a thronged tavern, dragging the slave behind him, talked to the bartender and passed through a door into the rear of the premises. Half-naked girls with garishly painted faces watched indifferently while the guard and brothel manageress talked.

'I do not buy slaves,' said the madam.

'She is young and comely. There are many years of labour in her.'

'She's lame. Let me see her walk. See! She can't hide it. But without the impediment I would still not buy her.' She gestured towards the patiently watching harlots. 'These earn well and divide with me. I do not have to *buy* them; and there are many others!'

The guard visited other brothels without success. Rome's lack of factories had caused great unemployment and none would buy a slave for prostitution when free women were available. But an innkeeper told the guard of a certain man. The man was sinister and his eyes glowed evilly when he looked upon the slave. He bolted the door of his shop against customers and led them into the back room. His sleeping palliasse was in one corner and a heap of mouldering straw in another. Chains bearing leather wristlets were stapled into the wall above the straw. On the walls hung whips and other instruments of torture.

'I would see her naked,' the man gloated and then devoured her with his eyes. 'I will buy her,' he decided instantly. He led the girl to the corner and reached for a chain.

The guard, a good-natured fellow, was sickened. 'She is costly,' he warned.

'We will not disagree,' the man answered and the girl shuddered as he passed a strap around her wrist.

'More than you will pay, I fear,' panted the guard.

'I offer forty sesterces!'

It was a good price. The guard had a duty to Brotan. But he'd seen this slave mature from childhood into a woman. 'Not enough,' he said and seized the girl's wrist to remove the strap.

The man stared in astonishment. 'Nobody will pay more.'

The guard dragged the girl back to the shop and as he unbolted the door the man said huskily. 'I *must* have her. What do you ask?'

'More than you can pay.' The guard was already thrusting the slave out into the street.

'One hundred sesterces!' shouted the man.

The guard's blood ran cold as he thought of Brotan learning of his treachery. 'Not enough!' he shouted back and almost choked the slave in his haste to drag her away.

He returned to Barba. 'Nobody will buy her.' he reported.

Barba sighed. 'Then Brotan must be content with what is paid on the auction block.' He ordered guards to lock her up with the other slaves.

The auction was held in a palm-shaded patio. Upholstered

benches were placed ready for the stewards who bought the slaves for their Masters' households. They were served wine and meat delicacies while the auction progressed.

Barba looked out upon his patio to learn if enough buyers were gathered to open the auction, stared hard and then licked his lips nervously, recognising among them a gay, golden-haired and handsome youth. Barba feared Saelig. He called guards and ordered them to stand ready to seize Saelig if he showed violence. He wondered at the young man's presence. What mischief was he about? Or did this young man who was once a slave, truly wish to buy his own slave?

Barba summoned up the courage to descend to the patio, seated himself between two guards and scowled when Saelig looked at him and laughed derisively, relishing his fear. To conceal his discomfort, Barba ordered the auction to begin.

Male slaves were sold first. They climbed the steps of a raised dais where they could be clearly seen and removed their tunics. The auctioneer turned them around and posed them while he drew attention to their best physical features. Farm-bred slaves always brought good prices. They were fourteen to sixteen years of age and trained for slavery. They had proper humility, were eager to serve and knew their status. Rome's prisoners of war, when sold as slaves, often lacked humility and nourished a resentment that had to be crushed.

The bidding was brisk. The large number of buyers provoked a competitive atmosphere. Barba's agents among them skilfully kept the bids climbing. It would be a good day, Barba realised. But he was uneasy about Saelig who occasionally shot Barba an amused glance yet took no part in the bidding.

But Saelig sat up with a buyer's interest when the female slaves were sold. The most comely was shown first and this girl was a great beauty. Her sackcloth tunic was not removed. Barba did not display female slaves naked. But they were available for private inspection by buyers on the day preceeding the auction. One good customer was eager to buy this slave for his master who had personally inspected and approved her. The bidding began at fifty sesterces and swiftly rose to ninety-five. The eager buyer tried to cut short the bidding. 'One hundred and fifty,' he shouted. There were sighs of awe. The auctioneer smiled and pointed at the eager steward, and then froze.

'A hundred and fifty five,' bid Saelig.

The steward turned red. 'One sixty.'

'Two hundred!' Saelig smiled and looked all around lazily.

The eager steward glowered as the slave was led away. His master would be angry. But perhaps his anger would be blunted by the second most beautiful slave. When the bidding reached thirty-five he shouted 'One hundred!'

'One hundred and five,' said Saelig.

The steward threw discretion to the wind. 'One hundred and fifty!' he bid recklessly.

'Two hundred,' said Saelig calmly and reached for his purse.

Barba fumed. His best client was being frustrated.

The steward was determined to buy the third slave. The moment bidding began he shouted 'One hundred!'

'And five,' said Saelig.

'One fifty!' stormed the Steward.

'And five,' smiled Saelig.

The steward looked as though he might burst. 'Two hundred!' he screamed.'

'And fifty,' said Saelig, and the steward threw up his hands.

Barba suspected then that in some devious way Saelig sought to destroy his business. He pictured Saelig recklessly buying all the slaves and disappointing all the other buyers. He was relieved when Saelig took no more part in the bidding.

The last slave was the lame girl. The auctioneer posed her skilfully but the buyers were not deceived. 'Both heels on the ground!' they shouted and the girl lowered her head in shame as a great howl of derisive laughter swept over her.

The bidding began at five sesterces and climbed slowly and painfully to thirty-five. There it stopped while the auctioneer tried to get another bid. Then Saelig said clearly. 'One hundred sesterces.' In the startled silence that followed the slave dared to look up; and her face was radiant.

Saelig arranged for his slaves to be housed and went about his affairs. He had been busy many weeks, performing at the theatre only occasionally, and devoting every other moment to a project that fascinated him. The estate agent thought Saelig was mad because many miles inland from Baiae, he had bought a large expanse of wasteland. The land was worthless, much of it being a lake and the rest honeycombed with waterways. It produced nothing except fish which could be caught with ease and in abundance in the river that flowed past Baiae.

Saelig then hired wagons and labourers and drove out to supervise the handsome villa being built alongside the lake. Even the labourers, who liked Saelig, thought he was mad. The residence was isolated, far from all social amenities and desolate in its loneliness. The labourers sighed with relief when they could return to busy, bustling Rome.

But Saelig's plans were ripening and when he received the message he awaited he rode to the port of Ostia. The docks were so full of craft being unloaded that many ships swung sluggishly at anchor in the bay. It was a colourful scene. Every type of vessel discharged cargo at the docks; huge fishing barges that had spent weeks at sea dwarfed the cockle-shell local boats with silver fish still leaping in their bilges. Diocles' new trading vessel dominated all others with it's three tiers of thirty rowing sweeps on either side, all new and gaily painted. Its towering mast would carry a vast expanse of canvas to drive it fast with a following wind. Its long, wide deck could be loaded high with cargo, and below deck much more cargo could be stored between the banks upon which sat the chained galley-slaves. Ships from the West and the East were gathered here; strange crafts, old and weather-beaten, burned white by the sun and looking as though they could not withstand a gentle breeze, much less the violent gales that often whipped the sea into clouds of white spray. And there were long, slim craft that slipped swiftly through the water and ranged the Mediterranean from end to end, trading profitably, bringing raw goods to Rome and bearing away its manufactured products.

Saelig met his man in a dockside tavern; a huge, black-bearded Moor with a strip of blood-red cloth wound about his head. He wore a large gold earring and had a sheathed, scimitar-shaped knife attached to the waistband of his pantaloons. He had his arm wrapped around a negress who clung to him affectionately, and he called for more wine the moment he saw Saelig.

'It was a good voyage?' asked Saelig.

'If the wind had blown hard your three hulks would have sunk!' The Moor guffawed. 'You are lucky; but my men are sad. To row and tow such heavy barges from the coast of Egypt with only a gentle breeze to fill the sail, was not to their liking.'

'I will reward them well.'

The Moor grinned artfully. 'First pay me the other half to complete our bargain.'

Saelig shook his head. 'First show me what you have brought!'

They went to the wharf and the Moor pointed to three barges moored at the mouth of the river. A small boat rowed them to it. They were large hulks, rotted with age and so low and heavy in the water they could easily be swamped. It was a miracle that they had survived the voyage. 'You have done well,' Saelig praised and the Moor grinned happily as Saelig counted coins from his purse.

The Moor's towing vessel was too big to serve Saelig's purpose and he chartered a small pleasure craft with six rowing sweeps. 'We will sail at noon tomorrow,' he told the Captain. 'Buy provisions and engage sailors.'

Saelig sent a messenger to Barba the slaver and the next morning two guards brought him his four slaves while the vessel was still loading. Barba had given them new collars and they were linked together by one rope. The rope-end was given to Saelig in exchange for his receipt.

The slaves were well-groomed and their sackcloth smocks newly washed. They stood with their eyes downcast, not presuming to look into the face of a master despite their burning curiosity to see their new owner. Saelig eyed them with compassion. They had been born into slavery and taught the passivity of dumb animals. Worse. Not even farm livestock would stand so still in blind obedience to rules. 'Follow me,' he said and led them across the narrow, wooden gangway. They quaked with fear of falling into the green water. None could swim. But they followed.

The vessel's passenger deck was strewn with cushions. 'Sit,' said Saelig. But the girls stood with heads lowered, unable to believe the order. A slave never sits in the presence of a master.

'Sit!' thundered Saelig. They started fearfully and, appalled by their action, lowered themselves on to the cushions. They sat bolt upright, their hands at their sides and their heads lowered.

Saelig was exasperated. He beckoned to a sailor. 'Remove their collars.' When it was done he told the girls. 'Raise your eyes. Look me in the face. It is an order!'

They were afraid to obey, but terrified to disobey. Their heads came up slowly. They stared into his face with blank, unseeing eyes.

'Do not call me master. Call me Saelig.' He waited for the shock of his order to sink in. Then asked. 'Tell me your names?'

They did not answer. Disbelief glowed in their eyes.

He pointed at one girl. 'Your name?' he demanded fiercely. 'No. Do *not* drop your eyes. Answer!'

Her lips trembled, her voice was inaudible. 'Number three seven two.'

'You have no names?' Their silence confirmed it. 'Then I will name you. And remember well your names.' He pointed to each in turn. 'Alpha, Beta, Gamma and Delta. Do you understand?'

They stared blankly.

'Answer!' he thundered. 'No. Do not drop your eyes! You! What is your name?'

They stumbled with the pronunciation; but he made them repeat their names until they spoke them correctly.

'Now. Who am I?' he asked. He made the terrified girls repeat. 'Saelig' again and again.

He looked into their faces intently. 'Smile!' he ordered.

They stared blankly.

'Watch me smile. Then smile as I smile!' When Saelig smiled it was as though a happy sun blazed down from a radiant blue sky, causing the world to laugh and sing with joy. Slowly the girls' solemn faces began to live. Their eyes brightened, their cheeks flushed and their lips quirked, unable to resist Saelig's infectious grinning. But their smiles were wiped away the moment Saelig ceased smiling himself. They sat stiffly erect, their eyes fixed upon him dumbly.

Saelig threw up his hands in despair. 'I'll have trouble making people of you. But you'll learn. Meanwhile, prepare food.'

This was an order they understood. They arose swiftly and fell over each other in their eagerness to serve in the tiny galley.

The Captain gave orders, mooring ropes were cast off and the little pleasure craft rowed out to the three anchored barges. It dropped two sailors on each barge and then took them in tow. The barges moved sluggishly despite the leverage of the sailor's long poles against the muddy river bed. But as they gained momentum they moved faster and the sweeps of the pleasure craft rowed up-river steadily. There was a favourable breeze and the Captain ran up a square sail. It billowed gracefully, a pleasing splash of rusted red against the greeny-blue water and the yellow beaches of the river.

Saelig relaxed on cushions while his slaves kneeled and offered him dishes without daring to look into his face. He admired their young loveliness but his eyes were sad when he saw how the collars they had worn since puberty had marked their skin. 'Look at me,' he ordered and when they obeyed he laughed and gestured they should feed him. But when they held delicacies to his lips he nibbled only a little and ordered. 'Now you eat. That is how it is to be. Always you will look into my face. And always you will eat when I eat.' He called the Captain to join them and his presence helped to ease the slaves' confusion. Saelig's eyes danced and he chided and teased the girls until they laughed despite themselves. Gradually a transformation overtook them. They became aware of themselves. They smiled and laughed ever more easily. They even allowed themselves to feel joy. Most of all they felt affection. It shone in their eyes when they had learned to look fearlessly into their handsome Master's face.

The voyage took many days. They branched away from the river into a tributary. It meandered lazily across country, looping back often upon itself so they travelled three times the distance they actually covered. Sometimes the river banks were so narrow the barges grounded softly on its sloping beaches, and once the bank had to be cut away before the barges could pass. The weather was fine and the voyage peaceful, birdsong mingling with the soft flapping of canvas and the rhythmic splash of oars. The girls worked with a will, eager to please. They cooked, served food, washed, cleaned and polished until the boat shone as though new. They were ever ready to leap forward to obey Saelig's slightest whim. His gay spirit imparted to them life of their own and within days they had shed their humility, called their Master Saelig, answered to their names and sat with him as though they were his equals.

At nights, when the moon glinted on the water and the vessel glided through the night to the sound of splashing oars, they reclined beside him, or sat silently while he sang in soft musical tones that moved them to sadness or joy.

They turned off from the tributary and entered a maze of waterways. The barges grounded often now and everybody dropped into the water and dragged the barges across the shallows after digging out a mud channel. Once, an entire day was spent cutting away a narrow bank that would not allow passage. The Captain voiced doubts the voyage could ever be completed. But Saelig had ridden on horseback to chart out this route and his confidence and enthusiasm encouraged everyone to labour willingly until the widening banks of a waterway opened out on to a lake. Saelig stood in the bows and pointed triumphantly to the opposite side of the lake. 'There our voyage ends!'

The lake was too deep for poling the barges but their momentum was easy to maintain by the oarsmen. Within an hour the barges grounded softly upon a shelving beach leading up to the terrace of Saelig's villa. Two female slaves came to meet them, wading into the water and welcoming Saelig by name. Saelig dropped overboard and gestured his four slaves to follow him. He half-lifted, half caught them and ushered them up the beach on to dry land. Then he pointed dramatically at his villa. 'Alpha, Beta, Gamma, Delta. Look upon your new home!'

Saelig's Farm-bred slaves felt they had been reborn into a paradise. Until they came to Rome they had never seen anything outside of Brotan's compounds. They marvelled at everything like new-born babies learning to live in the world outside the womb. The vastness of the countryside and its wild and varied colours delighted them. The beauty of nature was so moving it was music that blended with Saelig's singing and made them come alive. They were enchanted by everything, and all was new. Their five senses exploded into a new awareness that was intoxicating. Most important of all . . . they learned they were beings who could think, nourish desires and dislikes, and had the liberty to say and do what their emotions prompted. Freed from the restraint of rules, they exulted in the joy of living. All was magic. The food they ate was exotic and delicious. All their lives they had known only soggy rice and stale bread. Now, when they greedily crammed delicacies into their mouths, Saelig gave them laughing encouragement. They had worn only sackcloth but now owned tunics of fine cloth so delicately embroidered with coloured yarns that the thrill of personal adornment overwhelmed them. They had many tunics so they could wear all their garments freshly washed, unstained and sweet-smelling. From the other two slaves, Jaffa and Trenda, they learned the art of make-up, brushed and combed their hair until it shone silkily, smoothed their eyebrows into graceful arches, walked gracefully and proudly, instead of humbly, and learned to relish the natural beauty of their own bodies. The four had matured early. The eldest was only fifteen. So they could learn much more from the two slaves who would soon reach their twenties.

Although virgins, they had been taught all the ways to give pleasure to any master who would own them. But that had been slave disciplining. Their new freedom opened the floodgates to the loving, romantic emotions that seethe hotly within young girls. Until now, this had been crushed into a small kernel within them. But now they could love without restraint. They loved the lake, the fish that swam in it, the scent of pine cones, the songs of birds and the wayward clouds fleeting across the blue sky. They loved the grittiness of the warm earth they walked upon, the soft gurgle of clear stream-water flowing over stones, the magic sweetness of wine they had never before tasted, and the fragrance of the brightly-hued flowers that grew in abundance around the villa. They loved everything! And most of all they loved Saelig!

They worked hard, but work was a great joy. Their Master worked with them, sharing their labours and revelling in it, while his infectious laughter blended with their squeals of delight. But it was a new and strange work which they did not understand.

Saelig broke holes in the hulls of the partially beached barges below the water line. Then he stripped off his tunic and beckoned three of his slaves to follow him. They too stripped off their tunics, climbed aboard the barge and descended with him into the hold. They were knee-deep in mud that sucked at them tenaciously while they dug into it, sifting out the plants that thick mud had preserved throughout the voyage from Egypt. The barge held thousands of plants but Saelig was satisfied when only a hundred or more had been passed up through the hatch. Then they climbed out on deck, looked at each other and rocked with laughter. They were mud-daubed from head to toe, even their faces smeared black. Saelig pulled a shockingly ugly face, beat his chest with his fists and danced wildly like a jungle savage, convulsing the girls with laughter. Then with athletic grace, he leaped down into the water. His golden-brown body rolled over in the water like a basking shark's and when he stood erect again he was washed clean. 'Come!' he called. 'Time for baptism.'

They jumped into the water, sluiced themselves clean, splashed each other and laughed happily until Alpha stepped out of her depth. Her head disappeared and when it bobbed up she was gasping and splashing frantically. In a moment Saelig was with her, his strong arms bearing her into shallow water. 'Can you not swim?' he asked in astonishment, and when he learned that none could swim he began to teach them. The work was dangerous for all who could not swim, he warned.

They carried plants from the barge and stacked them in mounds at the water's edge. Jaffa, an Egyptian slave, supervised the work. She showed them how to plant them in clusters, and how lake mud should be scooped out and replaced with a mud-caked seedling brought from Egypt. All day they laboured, with interludes for mud-throwing and water-splashing, and intervals for swimming lessons. Soon all the girls could follow Saelig whenever he took a running dive into the lake and swam out into deep water.

The days passed blissfully. The planted seedlings were spread steadily around the lake where the water was shallow. The girls sang while they worked and happiness shone in their eyes. They had gained a confidence that showed in the carefree, graceful way they walked. Soon they believed they were . . . alive!

CHAPTER TEN

Areta too had been reborn through Saelig. His patient affection had made her realise that her selfish and madly possessive infatuation for him had made a monstrous woman of her. She still loved Saelig, but wisely and tolerantly now. She understood that the gay, irresistible Saelig overflowed with an abundance of love that no one woman could possess exclusively for herself.

Areta's passionate jealousy had almost destroyed her. Her folly was known to all and she would never return to Rome to face society's false welcome, and behind-the-back ridicule and scorn. Areta wanted to live alone and shun the world before it shunned her. But Saelig had proved to her that Rome's society was not the only world. He'd rented the villa next to hers, and Baiae took Saelig to its heart. His easy-going nature made him many friends, all doors were open to him and he made Areta cross their threshholds at his side. Baiae's wealthy residents had freed themselves from the pretentiousness of Rome, and despised it for a rabbit-warren infested with greedy merchants. Many learned men, teachers and philosophers had fled to Baiae, despairing of Rome's declining culture and its blood-thirsty mobs that howled incessantly for Circuses and bread. Baiae had also become the home of beautiful, sophisticated women whose married lovers found the attractions of their households in Baiae stronger than those in Rome.

At Saelig's side, Areta's dread of society's condemnation swiftly dissolved away. Her new friends scorned Rome's slavish subservience to Court etiquette, the fawning upon those of high rank, and the constant pursuit of social prestige. Women welcomed Areta with a warm friendship devoid of venomous gossip, and the malicious wish to tear someone to shreds. There were no jealous intrigues, nor spiteful plots to humiliate others and a complete lack of the wish to show off and make a public impression. For the first time in her life Areta found she could share confidences with friends she could trust implicitly. Most of them had escaped Rome's society protocol and rejoiced in its absence.

The men Areta met were easy-going, witty and entertaining. They shrugged their shoulders at trivialities that had seemed of immense importance in Rome, ridiculed the city's beehive activity, and scorned its self-important Senators and nobles who behaved as though they ruled the world.

Areta took a lover. He was introduced by Saelig, who with his understanding of people divined they would harmonise. Sark was five years younger than Areta and with her mature wisdom she could recognise his true worth. Sark was short and stocky. The girls he had wistfully pursued had looked down upon him mockingly while they'd subtly, and sometimes brutally, rejected his invitations. He was a noble's son, strong and vigorous, but strangely inept. When he wrestled he could always be thrown and no matter how desperately he concentrated, his arrows always flew wide of the target. When javelin throwing his spear always flew too far, or fell too short. He feared men's company because they used his clumsiness as a target for their cruel wit. All mocked him, especially the girls, until he made himself an outcast and lived within himself. When Sark's father died, leaving him a small fortune and a title, Sark sought again to get himself accepted. But nothing changed. Men taunted him for his lack of skill and girls spurned his rank and fortune. Sark turned to wild living. He frequented vice dens with ruffianly companions, his long nights beforgged by wine fumes and the sweat of harlots. He squandered money and lavished gifts upon all who showed him friendship. He gambled recklessly until

Postage
will be
paid by
licensee

No Postage Stamp necessary if posted in
Gt. Britain or Northern Ireland

BUSINESS REPLY SERVICE
Licence No. 9839

2

**CO-OPERATIVE INSURANCE SOCIETY LTD.,
MILLER STREET
MANCHESTER M4 8AA**

money was short, then sold his slaves and stripped his house of its furnishings. He eventually drank and gambled away his fine residence and the farm that was the last that remained of his inheritance. Saelig met Sark when he'd found a refuge as a stable-boy, living with warm-blooded animals that did not ridicule him. He shared their straw at night and groomed them by day. Saelig had sensed Sark's loneliness and the young man soon responded to his sympathy and poured out his troubles. Never before had anyone been willing to listen. They became friends and Sark visited Saelig in Baiae.

Sark had squandered a fortune. But he'd found common-sense. He was intelligent and educated, and entertaining if listened to. He hungered for affection and Areta was mature enough to ignore his short stature. She welcomed him warmly and was rewarded with an overwhelming flood of loving tenderness.

Areta was pleased when Hadrian visited her. She would never return to Rome, she told him. She was completely happy with Sark and she repudiated Rome's brittle society, which she had once believed so essential to graceful living. They agreed they had long ceased to need each other, but had been man and wife so many years they shared an affection and unselfishly wished each other to be happy. Hadrian talked of arrangements he would make to give Areta security. They did not consider divorce, which was an expensive formality. Hadrian agreed to employ Sark as one of his agents. He would work three days in Rome and then spend three days with Areta.

Then Hadrian told Areta about Haesel. She listened with barely concealed anger. A *slave*! What a blow to Hadrian's prestige and dignity! Any husband had the right to summon a slave and use her flesh to satisfy a momentary whim. But to feel affection for a slave, to treat her as a woman and break down the barrier between master and slave! It was unthinkable!

'What do you plan for this slave?' she demanded.

'We are lovers. I want her always at my side.'

Areta was furious. 'All Rome will laugh. You daren't set up a slave over your household. You will be mocked and ridiculed. The mob will shout after you in the streets!'

Hadrian was unperturbed. 'My dignity is my shield,' he said quietly.

She fumed because it was true. His integrity was beyond criticism. He was respected and whatever he did would be accepted as considered judgement, and not the stupidity of a vain man. Vicious tongues could wag but only to their own undoing. But Areta remained angry, thinking of the cunning slave who had shamelessly trapped an older man with her body. Men can always be fooled by young girls and become their tools, she thought. Now the little witch would artfully gain Hadrian's trust and bend him to her selfish desires. Worse! She'd usurp her mistress, occupy her mistress's bed-chamber and order Areta's slaves as though they were her own. Areta's cheeks flamed. When Poppea, Valle and her other friends learned how Areta had been usurped by a mere slave, their malicious tongues would flay her mercilessly. Areta drew a deep breath so she could explode into angry opposition.

Then, abruptly, all her rage drained away, leaving her calm and serene. For a moment, she'd been a woman of Rome. Now, with immense relief, she remembered she lived in a new world. And she thought of Saelig and remembered that she too had loved a slave.

'You are good, Hadrian,' she said softly. 'What you decide will be the best for everyone.'

Sark had become the hub of Areta's life. When he was away she visited and entertained extravagantly. But she was merely filling in time until Sark came home. He fulfilled her and she surrendered herself completely to this man who adored her so devotedly.

Occasionally, Areta went riding. She had not seen Saelig for many weeks and her curiosity was piqued. Why had he squandered a small fortune to build a residence in the wilderness? She had intended to call upon Elisa but on impulse she reined in her mount and wheeled it around. 'We will go *this* way,' she told the groom and he followed her when she trotted inland. But she'd ridden only a short distance when she reined in again. She didn't know where Saelig had built his residence. 'Leave me,' she ordered. 'I will return alone.' Without the slave's presence she would find her way without seeming foolish. It was easy riding on the hillside slopes, but in the valleys were rivulets of uncertain depth which she dared not ford. Often she circled around marshland, and two or three times she had to retrace her steps. She almost abandoned her plan but eventually crested a hill and looked down upon the lake and saw the villa Saelig had built. She approached it from the rear, dismounted, led her mount through closely clustered pines and tethered it behind the house. She called, but nobody came to meet her. She climbed the terrace, circled the house and from the front terrace saw Saelig and many laughing girls splash-fighting in the lake. She was tired after her journey and her riding chiton was damp with sweat. The terrace's reclining couches and cushions were inviting and she sank down with relief and enjoyed the cool shade. Presently the swimmers left the water and ran up the beach, the girls giggling explosively as Saelig whooped and slapped them playfully, herding them before him like sheep. Then he sprinted, his golden body a poem of athletic grace as he scaled the terrace steps many yards ahead of them. 'Greetings, Areta,' he welcomed her without surprise. The breathless girls wiped him dry and wound a loin-cloth around him. 'You will eat with us,' he said. 'Hurry,' he ordered. 'Prepare food for our guest.'

The girls pulled on tunics and hastened into the house. Saelig paced over to Areta and sank down beside her. He was a magnificent reclining animal.

'If you will not call upon me, I must visit you, Saelig,' Areta chided gently.

'I am honoured,' he said gallantly, seeming to make a sweeping bow without moving. He gestured, and sighed. 'The days pass swiftly and I have been busy.'

'Yes, Saelig. I can see that.' A soft smile played around her lips.

'And how is Sark?'

'As happy as he made me. He is industrious, serves Hadrian well and has gained confidence in himself.'

'I am pleased for you, Areta,' he said simply.

'And you, Saelig? What do you do so far from civilised life?'

His blue eyes danced. 'I serve Rome.'

'Here?' she doubted.

'Rome lives on papyrus, Areta. Papyrus is the blood that keeps the monster alive. It is needed for everything; bills of sale, accounts of debts, tax collecting, receipts, letters, permissions and official records. Without papyrus the monster will writhe in its last convulsion.'

'What has papyrus to do with you, Saelig?'

'Where do you obtain papyrus, Areta?'

She frowned. 'From a merchant.'

'But if they have no stocks, where do you then obtain papyrus?'

'I can never answer your riddles, Saelig. Where would I get papyrus?'

Saelig laughed infectiously. 'From me,' he said proudly. He gestured, embracing the lake. 'It is growing here at the water's edge, soon to glut the Roman monster with the blood it needs.'

'I do not see it, Saelig.'

'It is tender yet, Areta. But it grows strongly.' He laughed a welcome when the girls brought food and wine and set them down on a low table. 'Areta is a good friend,' he told them. They smiled at Areta warmly.

Areta was puzzled. The girls prepared food but did not show subservience. They sat with Saelig to eat, yet fed him soliticously as would slaves. Saelig offered food to them, as he did to Areta, and they responded fondly, often touching him with tender caresses. Areta became uneasy. The girls' richly embroidered tunics were of cloth too fine for slaves to wear and their nakedness in the water had revealed their body hair. Only outdoor slaves wore body hair, or mistresses who could indulge their whims. So they must be freewomen because no master could allow slaves such liberties. Yet, the girls' sun-tanned skin bore a dark imprint around the neck as though a slave's collar had indelibly branded them. Areta tried to engage Saelig in intimate conversation, but his gay answers embraced everyone and Areta constantly found herself in unwilling discussion with one of the girls.

The warm intimacy of the atmosphere was unmistakable and

Areta watched Saelig intently, weighing every word he spoke and wondering which girl he favoured. First, she thought it must be the Egyptian girl, then a dark-skinned beauty whose slanting eyes hinted at Oriental origin. He'd fondled her breasts when she leaned across the table and the girl had smiled with soft satisfaction. But they were all lovely and he favoured none. The comeliest girl limped, but despite her defect, Saelig stroked her hair fondly and she rewarded him with a smile of devotion. Areta fought against the growing suspicion that they were slaves whom Saelig had granted unbelievable liberties.

'When will you return to live in Rome, Saelig?' she asked, trying to cut him away from the others.

'The theatre pleases me less and less, Areta. Not the miming, which I enjoy. But the audiences, which I detest. I am unhappy in Rome. When I no longer need money, I will forsake the theatre entirely.'

She nodded approvingly. 'That is how it should be, Saelig. Spend more time in Baiae. Our friends constantly ask about you, and their households are ever-ready to give you welcome. You will die of boredom here. You must renew your social life in Baiae. Isolation will make you wither and dry up like an untended cabbage.'

He looked at her with sadness. 'I prefer Baiae to Rome, Areta,' he agreed.

'Rome is artificial. But Baiae is a new world,' she enthused. 'It is where *you* belong, Saelig.'

'My home is here, Areta.'

She stared at him disbelievingly. 'But what is *here*? What can you do?'

He chuckled. 'Our days are full. We tend our plants so they will multiply. And their essence will become the papyrus that Rome consumes so greedily.'

'Grow plants, Saelig?' she echoed disbelievingly. 'Like a peasant?'

Saelig laughed happily.

'Where are the workers who will make papyrus?'

'*We* are the workers,' said Saelig. He was amused at her incredulity, and beckoned. 'Come, Beta.' The girl arose and kneeled beside him. He raised her tunic and as she sat back on her heels he rested his hand upon the soft curve of her belly. 'We are the workers,' he repeated. 'And we will grow more workers!'

Areta saw the tell-tale thickening of the girl's hips. She glanced quickly to the others, looking for resentment or eyes sullen with jealousy. But the other girls looked upon Beta fondly, sharing her maternal joy as she would share theirs.

It was then Areta understood. Saelig could not live in Rome. Baiae, which was her world, was another in which he could not live. Saelig was building his own world in beautiful and natural surroundings. He was building a world that harmonised with his own gay unselfish nature; a world for only those who could share his love for all men, and within which jealousy, possessiveness, spite and hatred could not exist.

CHAPTER ELEVEN

At night Haesel went to Hadrian's bed chamber and nestled against him fondly, her breast warm upon his hip as she wound strands of her golden hair around him and made his maleness captive. 'I bind you to me,' she teased. 'Now, *I* am the master. You are the slave who cannot escape.'

'I am a willing slave. I want you always at my side.'

'Am I not always with you, Master?'

'Not as I would wish. I am master of a household. You must be its mistress.'

'To take the place your wife has abandoned?' she asked quietly.

'It is my wish.'

She was silent for a moment. 'I am a slave. I cannot be a mistress above other slaves.'

'It is my wish.'

'It is against reason and justice.' She giggled. 'Allow *all* your slaves to order your household.'

He sighed. 'Would you have me give them their freedom? They would despair. What would they do? Where would they go? Who would provide their lodgings and bread?'

She nodded wryly. She had learned painfully that most slaves were lucky to be enslaved. 'Yet I will not be their mistress,' she said decisively.

'I order it.'

'I am a disobedient slave, Master. Bind me. Whip me. Lock me in a dark cell without food or water. I will still defy you, Master!'

'There is another way,' he said. 'You will be mistress of your own household, to rule as you wish. There I will also have lodgings!'

'You have suggested that before. I do not want it, Hadrian.'

'What *do* you want?'

'I want you at my side, Master.'

'It is what I also want. But more. I want sons, borne of your loins.'

'I want it too, Hadrian. But only when it is time.'

'When?' he demanded impatiently. 'Why?'

'I am your willing slave. I share your work and dreams. We strive to make your dreams come true and I am content. I serve you, awake you, and bathe you; bring your breakfast, care for your garments, and when you are tired rub soothing oils into your weary flesh and wash from your feet the dust of Rome's streets.'

'These are slave's tasks,' he protested. 'They are not for you.'

She smiled. 'I am a willing slave. To serve you is my happiness. I would have it no other way.'

'And my sons that you must bear?'

'Later, Hadrian. Let us wait until Trebula is built. There you will have a fine villa. It is there I will give birth to your sons. Trebula will be a new way of life, Hadrian. There I can be mistress of your household. I will have slaves because it is the custom. And they will be content. It is not long to wait, Hadrian. When the villa is ready we will go to it. Until then, I will remain your slave in this household.'

'And if you conceive before Trebula is built?'

She smiled confidently. She had learned many secrets from other women slaves. 'We will see, Master. We will see.' She tugged strands of hair teasingly and then shuddered deliciously at the caress of his fingers upon her shoulder.

*

Poppea was furious. She strode her bed-chamber throwing cushions at the walls and lashing at wildly scampering handmaidens with her silver-hafted whip. All were nursing ugly welts. 'Where is the Head Steward?' stormed Poppea. 'Why doesn't he come?'

'Aloa is searching for him, Mistress,' said one handmaiden, then squealed as Poppea slashed at her.

'Why does he delay, girl. Go at once and bring him!'

Presently he came. He stood nervously upon the threshold, apprehensive of being slashed, but his dignity forbidding flight.

'Have you found him?' stormed Poppea.

'The household has been searched from top to bottom many times, Madam. He is not here. It is as I have told you, Madam. Strabo left the household this morning and has not returned.'

'Strabo would not disobey orders!' stormed Poppea. 'I sent him upon an errand from which he would soon return. He must be found or your hide will suffer!'

Strabo had been so recklessly favoured by his Mistress that all knew she was madly passionate about him. She'd betrayed her possessiveness in a thousand ways. That morning Strabo had been sent to buy a rare perfume that was an aphrodisiac. It amused Poppea that Strabo should encompass his own slavery.

But Strabo had not returned.

'Find him!' screamed Poppea, her tear-stained face ugly with frustration. Her whip hissed.

That morning, a freedman had stopped Strabo in the street. 'You are Strabo, of the Litirus household?'

'That is so.' Strabo was a slow-witted man, intent only upon his Mistress's order to hurry back.

'Your master awaits you,' said the freedman. 'I will take you to him.'

Strabo was confused by conflicting orders. The man showed him a paper. 'This is the written order of your master.'

Strabo could not read and stared at the paper blankly.

'Follow me,' said the man. 'Hurry. Your master is impatient.'

Strabo followed him reluctantly, plunging into a maze of narrow streets and becoming lost before he protested: 'My mistress also awaits me. She will be angry.'

'We are almost there,' said the freedman. He hurried him along another street and through a doorway. Strabo found himself in a simply furnished room. Another seated freedman rose to his feet. 'You are Strabo?'

Strabo nodded, looking around in bewilderment.

'Your master bids you wait. He has been called away but will return soon.' He pointed to a chair. 'Sit.'

Strabo sat. He had forgotten Poppea and was now fearful that he had angered his master. There was a flagon of wine and leathern cups upon the table. One freedman poured wine and handed a cup to the slave. 'Drink quickly before your master returns,' he urged.

Strabo gulped greedily. The wine was warm and heady. It had a piquant, syrupy taste. Before the cup was empty the freedman refilled it. 'Drink well, but quickly!'

Strabo gulped, and then wiped the back of his hand across his lips. The wine was strong and its potency swiftly spread across his chest and down to his abdomen. 'That was good,' he said with relish and became aware that the freedmen were watching him strangely. They had not drunk. Strabo frowned. His slow wits sensed the unusual. 'Where is my master?' he asked thickly. The wine was so strong it flushed his cheeks and roared in his ears. The freedmen were strangely blurred.

'Your master bids you wait. He will arrive soon.'

Strabo nodded slowly. A troublesome thought eluded him and the importance of remembering it dwindled as warmness lapped over his brain. Presently he slept.

When he awoke his senses were so addled it was long before he could make sense of his surroundings. He was compressed into a strangely shaped wooden box that smelled of tar and other vague odours. His head ached, his knees were under his chin and his head pressed against the top of the box. The strange rolling of the box helped him to realise slowly that he was a prisoner in the bilges of a ship. It seemed like days before he was released. Two powerful seamen dragged him up on deck and supported him while his eyes became accustomed again to the bright blaze of the sun.

'A stowaway,' one seaman reported to the captain.

Strabo denied it. But nobody believed him. He was given a choice. He could be thrown overboard, or could contract to work out the voyage. Strabo had little choice and made his mark on the contract.

'Where are we bound?' he asked as he was chained to a sweep.

'To all Mediterranean ports.'

'When do we return to Rome?'

'When the Captain decides.'

'What ship is this?'

'The finest. The biggest and newest in the Mediterranean. This is its first voyage. It was built by Patrician Diocles to voyage longer and farther than any other Roman ship.'

A whip cracked, fire cut into Strabo's back and he strained on his sweep. He had plenty of time to think. He thought of Poppea, remembered the two freedmen and their wine, and vaguely understood what had happened.

'I have a report from one of my ship's captains,' Diocles told Litirus. He smiled suavely. 'Not twenty miles from Ostia he was hailed by one of my outgoing ships and asked to report that a stowaway named Strabo had contracted to complete the voyage.'

'Strabo!' exclaimed Litirus. 'That scoundrel! Poppea's had the household in uproar, searching for the rogue. He must be mad to escape. He fared better than most slaves in other households.'

'What must be done?' asked Diocles blandly.

'I have posted him as an escaped slave, even though Poppea is convinced he would not run away. When he returns to Ostia he must be punished sorely.'

'I seem to remember him,' said Diocles thoughtfully. 'He is a big man?'

'As strong as an ox and as stupid,' agreed Litirus.

'He has contracted for a long voyage,' said Diocles thoughtfully. 'It is not justice that I profit from his labour. Shall I buy him from you? That will put an end to the matter.'

'A household slave is more valuable than a galley slave,' warned Litirus.

'Do not fear, Litirus. He is a powerful man. My captain will extract from him the full value of his labour. Are we agreed?'

'Agreed,' chuckled Litirus. 'I fear you have made a bad bargain. But I know you will regain your losses in other ways.'

'There *is* a licence I wish to obtain and which will richly line our pockets,' mentioned Diocles as he produced a contract for the sale of Strabo which he'd had prepared.

'We will keep this contract confidential,' said Litirus as he signed. 'Such an upheaval in the household because a slave escapes! Poppea is a tyrant about trifles when she believes her will is being opposed. Now peace reigns again, I have no wish to resurrect disorder.'

Alongside the swimming pool, young men and women filled the air with shouts of excitement as they ran, leapt, caught and threw a goatskin ball stuffed with goose-feathers. Two teams competed for a money prize and as they strove to score the most throws into the basket, sweat stained their tunics and dust billowed around their feet.

When the game of basketball ended, Marcus and Una sat on the edge of the swimming pool and splashed their feet in the water. Their flesh glowed warmly.

'You have great skill,' praised Marcus. 'You are so slim no one suspected you can throw so powerfully.'

Una laughed. She laughed easily now as though to compensate for the tragic days which she had firmly put out of her mind. 'It is not the throwing, Marcus. It is the way the ball is held before the throw. Your hand is big and you can grip the ball. Therefore, your fingers deflect it. Whereas, I hold the ball upon the palm of my small hand and can fling it with greater accuracy.'

'The ball should be bigger,' he mused. 'And it should be filled with sand. Then strength would be essential and men would not lose to women!'

'Must women *always* lose to men, Marcus?' she asked.

'They must, if men are to feel pride; and if women are to look upon them with admiration.'

'It is not for physical skill that women admire men,' she said quietly. She pulled off her tunic and her small, firm breasts glistened moistly. 'Women need tenderness too, Marcus,' she said, then slipped down into the pool, her hair streaming out like under-water seaweed as she swam down into the depths. Marcus plunged in after her, caught her and they laughed as they splashed and ducked each other. Then they left the pool and lay side by side in the sun while they dried.

'I must make a decision,' said Marcus. 'Much depends on you, Una.'

She turned on her side to face him, her eyes solemn. 'You wish to place a burden upon me, Marcus?'

He flushed. 'It is not my wish. But I cannot deny my heart. Together we have been happy, Una. I have watched you leave the shadows and begin to live again. We do everything together and laugh often. That is how we should always be . . . together!'

She lowered her eyes. 'I have asked you not to speak thus, Marcus. It is . . . too early. There is still a great sadness within me.' As she spoke she realised she ached for gentleness and warm protectiveness and remembered Hadrian who had given her these things. Then she thought of Juno who had given her a love that had made her truly come alive. Juno's death had numbed her senses; but dimly felt Marcus might be able to make her live again as Hadrian never could. 'Be patient, Marcus,' she urged. 'Give me time to find myself.'

He frowned. 'I wish to have patience, Una. But there is a matter I must decide now.' He plucked a grass stalk, chewed it and spat it out. 'There are many medical students in Rome. We work hard and earn little. It will be long before I'm respected and have wealthy clients.' He sighed. 'I do not complain. To heal the sick is rewarding. But now I have a chance to earn while I study. It is research work; not caring for the sick, but learning how man can grow healthy and be free from disease.'

'Then it is not difficult to decide, Marcus?'

'It is. To research I must leave Rome and sign a contract not to return for five years. Surgeon Malem wishes my answer now.' Marcus's face was pained. 'I will be torn in two if I do not see you, Una. I cannot suffer to be away from your side. Therefore . . . ' his voice turned husky. 'Therefore . . . it is in my mind to tell Surgeon Malem I have a wife who will lodge with me.'

There was a long silence. 'It is too soon,' sighed Una. 'I cannot leave Rome. I am rooted here. Perhaps already the roots are withering; but I have no wish to break them. It is . . . I need *time*!'

He rested his hand upon her hip. 'Do you believe you can be my wife? If so, I will be patient.'

She took his hand and pressed it against her. 'If *this* is what you want of me, you have your answer. But if you want more, I cannot tell you.' Her eyes searched his face. 'I cannot tell you what I do not know *myself*!'

'Then what must I do?'

'*You* must decide, Marcus. Take no account of me. Perhaps I will *never* change!'

Hadrian circled around the half-built villa followed by his Steward. The outer walls were now erected, showing it would be a magnificent residence. He climbed a ladder to the first floor and wandered from room to room, all open to the sky still. When he reached that intended for his bed-chamber he looked around approvingly. It would be spacious and well lighted. 'Where is the sculptor?' he asked. The man stepped forward, tanned almost black by the sun, but his long, corn-coloured hair a golden shawl upon his shoulders. Hadrian nodded to a steward. 'Note this carefully.' The man poised a stylo over a wax tablet.

'You are a Briton?' Hadrian asked the slave.

Thane nodded. He no longer resented his slavery; but it was not easy for him to be servile. Yet he did not need to be. Hadrian seemed unaware he was not answered with proper respect. 'You have memories of your homeland? The fields and trees, the dwelling huts of your people, the trades they followed, and their festivals?'

Thane's blue eyes shone. A man always remembers the land of his birth with pleasure. 'I do indeed,' he said softly.

'You are a talented sculptor,' said Hadrian. 'You shape stone into living beauty. Will you devote your skill to shaping beauty within this chamber?'

'I will, Sire,' said Thane huskily, caught up by Hadrian's enthusiasm, liking the man although he was a master.

Hadrian gestured at the walls of the chamber. 'I dream of this room lined with the sculptured beauty of Britain. It is a work in which you can excel yourself, Sculptor. Reproduce your native land. Depict scenes that make it memorable; its forests, its coast, men and women working in the fields, carts trundling to market and villagers celebrating a festival. Will you do this, Sculptor?'

Thane's eyes shone. 'I will do it, Sire!'

'And I will reward you well,' promised Hadrian. He paused, and then added. 'It is for a Briton; so she may awake with her eyes upon the memories of her country!'

CHAPTER TWELVE

Poppea's extreme of emotional hysteria were no more controlled than when she had been a spoilt child. She had cruelly vented her anger on all, becoming ever more violent as her frustration grew stronger. Then she'd collapsed and demanded ceaseless attention when her fears became reality.

She ached for Strabo and was tortured by fears for his safety. Had he been kidnapped by jealous rivals? Attacked by ruffians who'd cold-bloodedly murdered him for the expensive clothing he wore? Or had he fallen victim in a street brawl and been dragged away to prison? The search for Strabo was endless. The prisons were combed, inns and taverns searched, hundreds of citizens questioned, and reward notices posted. As the days passed Poppea's anxiety yielded to grief and despair, until finally a tiny seed of suspicion sprouted in her mind and grew rapidly. Strabo had vanished as though the earth had opened up to receive him. If he had died there would have been news of him by now; his giant body could not easily be concealed. If he lived he would be even more difficult to conceal, unless . . . ! Unless Strabo did not wish to be found!

The awful thought tortured Poppea. Into her mind crept a hundred little memories of how he had tried to evade her favours. He'd complained of headaches, hurried out eagerly on errands but dallied in returning. Many times she'd heard him sigh wearily at her insistent love-making. Had Strabo run away from her? Was Litirus right when he declared him an escaped slave?

The ugly suspicion flowered in Poppea's mind. She recalled hundreds of incidents that indicated Strabo had tired of her. It was a humiliating conviction she admitted only to herself. She, a mistress, had been scorned by a slave! He had taken advantage of the liberty she granted him to escape the city. Anger simmered within her and became a raging hatred. She marvelled she could ever have tolerated the stupid, oafish brute. She nourished her hatred with plans for his punishment when he was recaptured. Whips would flay flesh from his shoulders while she watched. His fingers would be broken one by one until his hands were insensitive lumps of flesh. And then her final revenge! He would be emasculated; shorn of his male brutishness. He would *never* know another woman!

But sweet though vengence might be, it could not fill Poppea's days. She was young and vivacious, thrived on flattery and ached to be admired. Her preoccupation with Strabo had made her neglect her friends and social obligations. She'd lazed contentedly at home with Strabo and dropped out of society. She realised now she had been out of her mind to destroy her social friendships for a passing infatuation. Now she was lonely. Worse. She was so cut off from her friends they no longer called on her, or sent her invitations. Even Diocles, an old faithful for whom she had great affection, had sensed her wish to be alone. He had not approached her for many weeks. There was only one friend to whom Poppea could turn. Melanos also had withdrawn from social life; but for different reasons.

Melanos received Poppea in a reclining chair. Her face glowed with a maternal radiance. She wore a loose wrapper she opened proudly, displaying the stretched skin of her belly. 'He'll be a fine, strong boy,' she told Poppea contentedly. I'm eating like a horse.' She gazed down upon herself fondly and a soft smile touched her lips.

'I'm sure he will be,' said Poppea formally. 'He'll take after his mother.' She settled down on a reclining couch and nibbled the sweetmeats slaves placed before her. 'I need your help, Melanos,' she said bluntly.

Melanos looked up, unwillingly turning her thoughts away from maternity. She was shocked by Poppea's appearance. She'd always been gay and vivacious. Now she was pale and the strain of conflicting emotions had pinched and drawn her face. Her eyes were pools of anxiety. A wave of sympathy swept over Melanos. She was so happy herself she wanted all others to be happy too. 'What is it, Poppea?' she asked with an understanding that brought a flood of confidences from Poppea.

'I have been foolish, Melanos,' admitted Poppea. 'You may have heard rumours?'

Melanos suppressed a smile. Every detail of Poppea's infatuation with Strabo had been discussed by her slaves and passed on to slaves of other households. Confined to her home, Melanos had been greedy for gossip. Her handmaidens might have been eye-witnesses judged on the vividness of the tales they'd told.

'In a weak moment I allowed my emotions to dominate my common sense,' Poppea admitted. 'I should have known better. Strabo is a brute; an animal!'

'But a magnificent animal,' Melanos said softly.

'Perhaps,' agreed Poppea grudgingly. 'But witless.' She became querulous. 'It's always difficult with slaves. If you allow them a little liberty, they abuse it. I blame myself. I should never have given him a momentary favour. But because of that moment of weakness he became increasingly disrespectful. Finally, I told him I would report him to Litirus. He realised he'd gone too far. He's a coward. He went down on his knees and pleaded with me for forgiveness. But I was adamant. Litirus is not a stern master, but Strabo's flogging would have been severe. Despite his strength, Strabo is a coward. He was terrified of Litirus and ran away.' Poppea shrugged her shoulders to show her indifference. 'That saved a great deal of trouble.'

'It must have been a great relief for you,' consoled Melanos. She'd been told how Poppea had screamed, lay on her bed, torn her hair and wailed despairingly when she'd learned Strabo was missing.

'To run away is unforgivable,' said Poppea. 'When he is recaptured I will urge Litirus to punish him severely.' Her eyes glowed. *'Severely!'* She looked as savage as a cat stalking a mouse and Melanos suppressed a shiver. But the next moment Poppea said casually. 'With these problems of disobedient slaves I haven't felt well these past few weeks. I haven't been out or seen anybody!'

'I sometimes have visitors,' mentioned Melanos.

'But I have none,' wailed Poppea.

'Go out more, Poppea. You are young and gay. I am content to take my ease in the garden.' Melanos rested her hands delicately upon her swollen belly. 'But you need friends and excitement.'

Poppea nodded. 'This is why I come to you, Melanos. I've neglected my friends. But I am too timid to take up with them again. I need your help.'

Melanos instantly understood. Poppea was unsure of herself. She'd been humiliated and her pride had suffered. She'd lost her courage and feared a social rebuff.

'How can I help, Poppea?'

'It is natural for you to dine at home. If you invited me and some of our friends . . . ?' Poppea's voice tailed off miserably.

'A lovely idea!' said Melanos. 'A pregnant woman is self-engrossed and boring to others. But you *will* come, won't you, Poppea? And who else? Who do you suggest?'

Poppea smiled, almost the gay and light-hearted Poppea of old. 'Diocles is always so laugh-provoking,' she mentioned. 'And he'll be sure to invite me to other parties!'

'Alone? Or with Valle?'

'Wives can be *so* frustrating,' mused Poppea. 'Valle *does* keep interrupting Diocles.'

'Diocles, then,' agreed Melanos. 'And who else?'

Poppea stared straight at her. 'Do *you* wish to invite anybody?'

Melanos chuckled. 'Who will whisper sweet endearments to me at an intimate dinner party?' Then she became thoughtful and her eyes glowed. 'I will amuse myself, Poppea. I will invite Alexander!'

Poppea was astonished. 'Do you think you should?'

'To tantalise him, not to satiate him,' explained Melanos. 'I will cover him with confusion.'

'There will be wine to warm Diocles' blood?' asked Poppea, so Melanos would have no doubt what she wanted.

'Strong, rich wine,' confirmed Melanos. She too had known the frustration of long lack of sexual satisfaction.

'And . . . perhaps a spectacle?' Poppea suggested shyly.

'Have no fear. Diocles will be provoked,' Melanos promised.

When Poppea left, Melanos summoned her handmaidens. They gathered around her, clucking like hens as they planned the dinner party for Poppea.

'And you, Mertice,' said Melanos. 'You will be revenged upon Alexander.'

Mertice's eyes widened. 'I do not hate Alexander, Mistress.'

'Do you not wish him to hunger for you, as you have hungered for *him*, girl!'

Mertice flushed. 'It would not be possible.'

'But it would please you?'

'Yes, Mistress.'

'Then we shall see. You are my companion. You will sit with me at dinner. I am too swollen with child to be a good hostess. You will preside in my place.'

Mertice's face showed her consternation. 'I *couldn't*, Mistress. I am a slave. It would not be seemly. I would not know what is expected of me.'

'Nonsense, girl. You are a slave and will obey my orders. You will be Mistress in my place. You will dress in fine clothes and be as proud and arrogant as a Mistress.'

'But . . . ' wailed Mertice.

'Silence. It shall be as I order. If Alexander is not a bigger fool than I believe, he will lose his head.' Melanos gave her hands to her hand-maidens to be pulled to her feet and then stared down happily at her swollen abdomen. 'How would I look astride a horse?' she chuckled, and the handmaidens laughed with her.

CHAPTER THIRTEEN

Alexander was at first intrigued by Melanos' invitation. He had not seen her for many months but when he reckoned up and realised her time was almost due he understood. She would be conscious of her appearance and unwilling to go abroad. He wondered if motherhood had changed her views on marriage? They would be a good match, he mused. Their joint fortunes would give time influence and power. And he had always admired Melanos despite the disconcertingly mocking attitude she adopted towards him. She was exasperating, sometimes praising him so lavishly he suspected she mocked him. Perhaps her taunting was meant to provoke him to attentiveness. His dignity could not permit him to yield to a woman. But if Melanos . . . !

Alexander's discreet enquiries showed that none of Melanos' other friends had been invited, and expecting it to be an intimate dinner there were many half-formed plans seething in his mind when he was received by Melanos head steward. His formal toga was removed, he donned a comfortable tunic and only when he reached the dining chamber did he realise it was not what he'd expected. Poppea, looking as haggard as a witch, reclined opposite Diocles, a man for whom Alexander had no liking. Diocles was a middle-aged clown with more words than a lawyer and a disconcerting knack of gaining everyone's attention when he mouthed witticisms that made no sense to Alexander. Melanos was not reclining. She sat sprawled on a low chair, her grossly swollen belly freezing all his romantic ideas. Her graceless posture showed her complete indifference to his good opinion. Reclining beside Melanos, was a lovely, blue-eyed girl with long blonde hair. Alexander recognised the girl but could not place her. Nor did Melanos mention the girl's name when she gestured him to take the reclining couch opposite her.

The feasting had already started. Diocles had broken off momentarily from a joke he was recounting, and not understanding its point, Alexander was unable to join in the gale of laughter that greeted it. A serving girl poured wine, wiped his lips with a napkin and then placed savouries upon his tongue. The serving slave was attractive but he resisted the casual impulse to fondle her. Melanos had strange ideas about what she called *'men's primitive passions'* and had provided single instead of double reclining couches. He guessed that Diocles and Poppea were discomfited. They talked animatedly, thrilled to be with each other. But they had so often shared a couch while feasting that they must miss the piquancy of intimate bodily contact.

'Fill Alexander's cup,' ordered the blonde girl. 'Keep it filled,' and as the serving-girl hastily obeyed, Alexander smiled his thanks at the girl acting as hostess.

She smiled slightly and her blue eyes stared into his disconcertingly. He was embarrassed that he could not recall her. He knew her well; but where and when they'd met escaped him. He saw that her white chiton was so finely woven that her warm flesh glowed through it. She wore jade earrings, a necklace of pearls and ruby-studded bracelets upon her arms. Her fair eyebrows lent themselves to make-up which had transformed them into intriguingly arched scimitars. Her eyelids were coloured turquoise-blue and sprinkled with gold-dust.

'Did we meet at a Court reception?' Alexander asked casually.

There was a ripple of mocking laughter from Melanos. 'He is *so* ungallant, Mertice. He doesn't remember where you met. Don't yield to his curiosity.'

Alexander glowered. Melanos could always read his thoughts and thwart him. But at least he knew the girl's name. 'Caesar always invites many guests, Mertice,' he apologised. 'Forgive me that I forgot your name. But your beauty has lived with me and I knew you instantly.' He became aware that Poppea and Diocles were listening intently, and there was a glint of ridicule in Poppea's eyes that made him uneasy. Diocles grinned broadly, his fat face comical and mischievous.

'I forgive you, Alexander,' said Mertice with dignity.

'You are *too* popular, Alexander!' said Diocles. 'Rome's loveliest women beseige you in such profusion you cannot remember them all.'

Poppea squealed with laughter and suspecting Diocles had spoken with double meaning Alexander glowered sulkily and gulped wine. 'You humble me before Mertice,' he complained.

'But if Mertice is to forgive you,' said Diocles innocently, 'it is just that you humble yourself to her.'

Alexander seized the opportunity Diocles gave him. 'Allow me to redeem myself, Mertice?' he pleaded. 'To gain your good graces I will devote myself to pleasing you.'

'Mertice is very demanding,' interjected Melanos. 'Take care Alexander, lest her beauty makes a slave of you.'

He knew from their secret smiles that all mocked him when Mertice asked softly. 'Do you wish to be my slave, Alexander?'

'I yearn to be your slave, Mertice,' answered Alexander gallantly. 'Any man would be proud to be allowed to be at your side.'

Mertice's eyes were warm and tender and he knew she was captivated by him. But the others subtly thwarted his verbal flirting with Mertice, even quickly answering questions he asked her, before she could reply. He sensed they were subtly taunting him but he remained dignified and composed. He could afford to because Mertice held his eyes, smiled and showed in every way a woman knows, that she looked upon him favourably. The wine was rich and warming, his blood glowed and Mertice became ever more lovely and inviting. He admired her breasts shimmering beneath her transparent gown and felt the warmth of them stir his loins, and in the way she smiled upon him. He was pleased Melanos had arranged a spectacle while they feasted. It aroused an atmosphere of sensual intimacy. The two girls were in their twenties. One was coal-black and the other blonde and with milk-like skin. Their nudity made startling contrasts as they wrestled. But it was symbolic wrestling. Their limbs curled around each other with the bonelessness of snakes, and as they writhed sinuously their greedy mouths lasciviously sought lesbian rewards. They loved with the magic of woman's tenderness and as Alexander watched them, enraptured, the serving slave replenished his wine as quickly as he drank it. He glanced up often at Mertice and her answering smile promised they were intimately united by the visual sensual stimulation they shared.

Hot desire flushed through Alexander's mind and he was disappointed when the exhausted wrestlers withdrew, and was surprised that dinner was over. Time had flown. Poppea and Diocles bade him goodnight. They went upstairs and when Poppea took Diocles' hand, his arm slipped naturally around her waist. Her rippling laughter sounding from the floor above was cut short by a closing door.

'It is time to retire, Alexander,' said Melanos pointedly. Her handmaidens pulled her to her feet. Alexander arose, his hot eyes upon Mertice and her answering smile was an invitation. Melanos opened her chiton and stared complacently at her swollen belly. The flesh was so distended that blue veins marbled it. 'Do you still adore me, Alexander? With my belly swollen like a bullfrog?'

'I always adore you,' he answered dutifully.

'You flatter me too much, Alexander.' Melanos giggled, turned away and ascended the stairs slowly. Mertice followed her without another glance at Alexander. He stood irresolute, not knowing what was expected of him. Then Mertice smiled at him softly over her shoulder.

Alexander waited discreetly before he followed them. Melanos, surrounded by handmaidens, entered one bedchamber; Mertice entered another. He stood on its threshold and watched Mertice seat herself before the polished metal that showed her reflection. She relaxed dreamily while handmaidens removed her jewellery, and her robe, washed the make-up from her face and brushed her hair. A slave sprinkled fragrant perfume around the room and another scattered flower petals upon the bed.

'You are lovely, Mertice,' said Alexander, his voice husky.

Her eyes turned to him, she smiled and turned away.

He approached her slowly, drinking in her radiant, soft-skinned loveliness. 'All this night my thoughts were only for you, Mertice,' he whispered.

She studied her reflection in the mirror. 'It is pleasant to hear praise upon your lips, Alexander.' She reclined back so the long brushing strokes of her handmaidens could make her hair shine like silk.

He approached closer, almost touching her. 'You have addled my senses, Mertice,' he said thickly. 'To look upon your beauty makes my bones weak. You have bewitched me.' He fondled one cool, firm breast and thrilled when the nipple instantly tautened. But handmaidens busily intervened, delicately shouldering him away so they could massage aromatic oils into their mistress's skin. Alexander stepped back and controlled his impatience while he feasted his eyes upon Mertice. 'I will love you to distraction,' he promised. 'I adore you. You have enslaved me!'

When at last the handmaidens had prepared their mistress she arose and they clustered around her as she moved to the bed. They helped her repose and adjusted the sheets around her. But when Alexander would have approached Mertice, the handmaidens formed a barrier between them. They were giggling.

'What is this, Mertice?' asked Alexander, bewildered. 'Will you send away your slaves?'

She smiled softly, her blue eyes full of promise. 'I am tired, Alexander. I would sleep, *now*.'

He could not believe his ears. He made to step forward but the handmaidens clustered more closely together.

'Alexander is leaving,' Mertice told them. The slaves giggled explosively as they moved forward, protecting their mistress from him, and urging him outside. For a wild moment he was tempted to strike them. But brawling with slaves was unthinkable. He turned on his heel and strode out, raging with frustration. When he reached Melanos' bed-chamber his cheeks flamed as the giggles of the handmaidens followed him along the corridor.

Melanos was still at her toilet. She looked up without surprise, as though expecting him. 'You are very flushed, Alexander,' she said. 'Are you over-heated?'

He glowered. 'What does this mean, Melanos? Mertice looked upon me fondly. Perfume was sprinkled and flower-petals were scattered upon the bed. Yet I am sent from her bed-chamber without being favoured!'

Melanos looked down at her swollen belly and stroked it tenderly. 'Perhaps Mertice does not wish you for a lover.'

He scowled. 'She has aroused a fire in my loins that must be quenched.'

Melanos looked at him wickedly. 'For this reason you come to me, Alexander?'

'Who is she?' he demanded. 'Why does she slight me?'

'You do not remember her, Alexander?'

'How could I forget such beauty?'

'But once you marred it. You sheared off her hair and made of her a ridiculous spectacle at the Baths.'

Alexander stared at her. His memory was triggered. A bald-headed slave who'd wrestled and lost him a wager; a slave Melanos had won with a luck bolt from a bow. His face turned grey. 'It was *her*!' he whispered.

'It is Mertice,' said Melanos calmly.

'You've made me humble myself to a slave!' he choked.

'You humbled yourself to beauty, Alexander.'

'You dressed her in rich clothes, surrounded her with handmaidens and gave her authority no slave should possess!'

'She is my companion and my friend, Alexander. She is also a slave.'

'You have tricked me!' he stormed. 'It was a plot to humiliate me!'

'Are you angered that a slave rejects you, Alexander?' Melanos asked sweetly.

'*This* is unforgivable, Melanos!' He stormed from the room, the wine running so hotly in his veins he cuffed the slaves who escorted him to the door. His litter-bearers were waiting patiently and he tongue-lashed them as he was borne through the night streets. His anger pulsed in his blood and loins. Again Melanos had made a fool of him; and it hurt. *Now* he understood Poppea's squeals of merriment and the double meaning of Diocles' words. But even as wrath burned in him, another awareness burned as strongly. Mertice's beauty haunted him. Her blue eyes and warm smile invaded his thoughts. Only the delicate symmetry of her body could assuage the ache of his own. He *must* possess her, he vowed. And when his hunger was blunted he would take his revenge at leisure, submit her to much worse humiliations than he had suffered.

Alexander relaxed and the anger drained out of him as he planned his revenge. He would pay the price Melanos asked for the slave, even if it cost the equal of three or four trained chariot horses.

The slave was truly lovely and he was impatient to possess her. If she pleased him, he might not treat her *too* harshly, he decided.

Melanos and her handmaidens giggled long after Alexander had flung out of the room.

'Mertice was very convincing, Mistress,' said one handmaiden. 'But I fear she secretly yearns for him.'

Melanos sighed. 'It is hard for a woman to reject the man she favours.' She gestured. 'Greta. Hurry and bring Steward Octavius. Tell him to attend upon Mertice this night. She has savoured revenge. But has tormented her own desires, I fear. She has need of Octavius.'

Hadrian climbed steps he knew well but had not seen for many months. He was expected. A handmaiden led him straight to Una's bed-chamber. She arose swiftly, ran to him and rested her cheek upon his chest while his arms enfolded her. It was a warm reunion, their natural fondness flooding out with great tenderness. He sat beside her on her sleeping couch while her handmaiden served food and drink. 'You are beautiful, Una,' he said quietly. 'But a shadow overhangs your beauty. You have suffered much?'

'The pain has left me,' she said quietly. 'The wound is numb. But it is still not healed.'

'I would have come earlier if you had sent for me,' he said simply.

'I know. But the passing of Juno was a loss I had to bear alone. You could not have helped, Hadrian. You could not give me what his passing took away.'

He nodded understandingly.

'For a time I did not wish to live,' she admitted.

'But you were not alone in your misery,' he said gently.

She smiled tenderly. 'Then you know about Marcus?'

'Even though we do not meet, my fondness for you is strong. I receive regular reports so that I know you are well.'

'Marcus helped me. In my grief I did not know it. But he was always at my side, gentle and affectionate, caring for me and giving me the will to live again.'

'You cannot live in the past, Una. You must live *now*, and in the future; and *for* the future.'

'That is why I sent for you, Hadrian.' Her eyes were upon him, solemn and trusting. 'I have need of you.'

'If you have need of me I am pleased, Una.'

'I need your strength, your affection and your comfort so that I do not live alone.'

'And what of Marcus?' he asked gently.

She looked down at her hands. 'I am not yet alive, Hadrian. Part of me is numb. I cannot know what it is I want.'

'Do you love Marcus?'

She looked up, took his hand and placed it upon her, pressing his fingers until they moulded to her flesh. '*This* is the love I can share with Marcus. But *this* is not all of love. There is another love which is not of the body, and to this I am numb. Perhaps I will live again and know this love anew. Perhaps I can share it with Marcus. But perhaps I cannot. Therefore, I have sent him away.'

'Was that wise?' he asked, after a pause.

'It is wise for Marcus. He must choose to remain in Rome, or to make a new way of life. I will not influence him. He has called many times but I refuse to see him ever again. He knows now I am determined. Therefore, he can choose freely.'

'A decision you may regret,' he warned.

'If my heart tells me, I will seek him out. Even if he is far from Rome I will find him. Already I feel sadness, Hadrian. The sadness for an absent friend. Therefore I need you, Hadrian. Be my comforter. Call often, talk with me, show me I am admired, and loved with the fondness we share. Help me dispel the loneliness I suffer now Marcus no longer fills my days.'

Hadrian stroked her hair. 'I will call often, Una. We will laugh and talk with optimism.'

She rested her cheek upon his chest. 'And you will give me comfort, Hadrian? The warm comfort of unselfish affection?'

CHAPTER FOURTEEN

Brotan was deeply disturbed. He did not understand himself. For years he had devoted himself to breeding with eager enthusiasm. And now, abruptly, he had lost interest in the Farm. It was as though an exotic delicacy had turned to ashes in his mouth. He no longer made his rounds with an eagle eye, alert for slackness or wastefulness. Smooth and efficient production no longer thrilled him. Instead, he'd grown increasingly and sickeningly aware that his world was crammed with women, Women, WOMEN!

Brotan broodingly remembered that his apathy had begun a few days ago when three incidents had occurred on the same day. They were trivialities which normally he would have dealt with as routine. But coming together, the incidents had made bigger impact. Perhaps they were straws that broke the camel's back, he wondered? He rose to his feet and paced the room angrily, furious with himself without knowing why. Life had always been exciting and full. Suddenly, it was empty and dreary. Merely to think of the herds of women that surrounded him was nauseating. He realised he hungered for something different, but did not know what it was. He was still pacing the room when a serving girl brought a tray of food and drink. The sight of her nude body, downcast eyes and humility enraged him. He smashed the tray from her hand, knocked her to the ground and kicked her repeatedly.

The first upsetting incident had been brought to Brotan's attention by Surgeon Malem. He'd displayed a small object. 'Look at this!' he'd said with dramatic incredulity. 'LOOK!'

Brotan examined the object with distaste. 'What is it?'

The Surgeon spluttered in agitation. 'An appalling concoction. Wood-ash, boiled rice and cattle dung, for all I know. Pounded into a paste and kneaded together with flax-fibre!'

'But what *is* it?' persisted Brotan, eyeing the exhibit dubiously.

'A contraceptive,' said the Surgeon.

There was a long silence.

'The guards reported it,' explained Malem. 'I investigated. The women must be out of their minds. Our work is being *disrupted*!'

The second incident had been much more important. Slave Number 122 had all the hallmarks of a breeder to Malem's experienced eyes. Malem had changed his usual routine and sent her to be fertilised a third time. He'd ordered her to be served by many guards. This was the slave who loved her master, whose child she'd borne, and who yearned to return to him. She'd dreaded conceiving again and had *willed* her body to resist conception. But her third visit to the guards had brought results and after three months' weaving in the factory, Malem had made a routine examination and smiled satisfaction. 'This one is pregnant,' he'd told the overseer.

The slave had been transferred to the maternity compound where she washed, cooked and cared for the infants. But her heart ached and she cried herself to sleep at night. She pined for the kindly master she loved, and to whom she had hoped to return when her contract expired. But now she would bear another child, and perhaps a third. Her young beauty would be ravaged by child-bearing until she could not please her master, even if she did return to him. Every day she saw breeders with elastic-skinned bellies unashamedly distended, or else stretch-scarred with wrinkled flesh hanging in limp folds awaiting the next pregnancy. She saw the feeders lazing in compulsory idleness, dedicated to producing abundant milk, constantly caring for tender nipples made huge and long by incessant suckling.

And when, in these women, she saw her own future, the anguish within her swelled up overwhelmingly until she was choked and her body racked with silent sobs.

In her sixth month she was examined again by Malem. He held her breasts as though weighing them, stretched out their nipples and nodded approvingly. His dark, harassed face brightened with a smile of satisfaction. He ran his hand down over her swollen belly and his sensitive fingers probed knowingly. He nodded his head. 'This will be a big baby,' he told his assistant. 'Excellent! It just kicked vigorously!'

His hunch had paid dividends and he couldn't resist boasting. 'This slave will make a fine breeder,' he said confidently. 'She's young. We'll get at least a dozen out of her.'

This was when a wave of mingled anguish and fury overwhelmed the slave. She hit out blindly. Malem staggered back, his face showing complete amazement. She went after him, hitting again and again until he tripped and went down before her. She went down after him, still hitting and hitting until many hands pulled her away.

Malem was more shocked than hurt. A few bruises were of little significance compared with the magnitude of the slave's offence. A slave should not even dream of hitting a master.

The third incident was more serious than the others.

Slave Number 287 had once been in the household of an elderly Patrician who allowed his slave great liberties. They lived well, ate plentifully and their varied duties were light. Games and recreation were encouraged. It was a happy household until the elderly master died. His son, who already possessed a fine household, put his father's property up for sale. Slave 287 was sixteen when she was bought by a mean merchant who worked his slaves hard, fed them little and imposed stern discipline. The girl could have withstood this. But she was attractive and on her first night the master had had her brought to his bed-chamber. He was an energetic man easily annoyed by even the petty annoyances that accumulated during the day, and which he dispersed by night. He assailed the girl's body with bad-tempered vigour. He ignored her fatigue and by day she laboured as hard as the other slaves, and his nightly invasion of her body became torment. Her nerves screeched at the mere thought of his touch. She was goaded to attempt escape. She was easily recaptured, whipped soundly and sexually used by her master with increased vigour.

It was a happy escape when her condition brought her to Brotan's Farm. But the child was still-born and when she'd recovered she was sent to the guards. The touch of their hands rasped upon her nerves like sandpaper upon raw flesh. Their male invasion was unbearable and she resisted them frantically. So they bound her and punished her ruthlessly with the weapon they'd learned tormented her most. Then, when it was over, she was taken to the weaving factory. She dreaded being sent to the guards again and devised a wild plan. Her fingers fumbled clumsily with yarn and the cloth she wove had to be unravelled. She was transferred to outdoor labour. She bided her time. Every morning the overseer awakened the slaves by cracking her whip; they ate, then stood in line while a rope was passed through the rings in their neck collars. They waited then until a guard led them out to the fields. The work was hard but the slave was wiry and accustomed to labour, and while she worked she was strengthened by her dream of escape. She observed how the guards often dozed in the sun while the slaves dully continued their labours in blind submission to authority. She became adept at being the last girl in line and it became routine that when they were marched off to the fields, she was the end girl. The opportunity came when she was working in the rice-paddy. The guard was asleep in the shade of a tree. She was the farthest from him. The slaves worked at the edge of the paddy within easy reach of sheltering bushes and shrubs. As the slaves stooped with the sun blazing on their backs, the slave untied the rope that linked her to the others. When she was free, she lowered the rope into the water, weighted it with mud to keep it taut and slipped quietly into the bushes. She ran madly. Her one thought was escape. She ran until her heart pounded painfully, till she was ready to drop, yet still kept running. She ran with desperation a long, long time before she dropped exhausted into concealing scrub. Her feet were torn and her legs bloody from the thorns and thistles that had slashed them.

She lay a long time before she sat up and sent a searching glance all around her.

She was alone in the midst of scrubland that stretched as far as the eye could see, except for a tree-lined hill slope, many miles away. When she could, she climbed to her feet and limped towards the hill, often sending fearful glances over her shoulder.

She reached the hill and rested in the shade of closely-growing pine trees. Only then did she realise she had not planned enough. She was naked except for her collar; hungry, foodless and not knowing in which direction to escape. She foraged for nuts and berries but found none. She scaled the hill, descended the slope the far side and found herself facing another large expanse of scrubland with a hill in the far distance. She was thirsty but the soil was parched. She made the distant hill a landmark and set off towards it. It was farther away than she realised. After walking a long time it was still no nearer. Yet the hill she had left behind looked equally far away. Her feet were blistered, sweat stung her lacerated flesh and her tongue was dried leather. Lizards scattered at her approach and she screamed when a yellow-striped snake glided away as she was about to step upon it. The sun blazed down remorselessly and her head ached intolerably. She no longer looked behind her in fear of recapture. She stumbled on blindly and purposelessly.

She reached the hill as the sun was going down. She had a raging thirst and was weak with hunger. She sucked a dry pebble, encouraging saliva to moisten her mouth, then a pine cone that oozed a liquid with a disgusting taste. She gathered pine needles to make a bed but she slept fitfully. She longed for the warm straw of the farm and shuddered as insects crawled over her and stung her flesh. The night was filled with scuttlings and slithering and eyes that glowed luminously. At dawn she crawled into the scrub, sucked yellowed grass stalks and extracted a little moisture from them. Then she stumbled on again, walking aimlessly, no longer trying to escape but instead hoping to be found. The will to live is strong and all other fears are diminished by it.

It was afternoon when she reached a green valley with cultivated fields. She dug up a turnip and its juicy crispness gave her a little strength. She feared to spend another night in the open and stumbled on until she saw a man working in a distant field. She turned her dragging steps towards him.

Presently, the man saw her. She stumbled twenty paces, sank down on her knees to rest, arose and then stumbled on again. The man untethered his donkey and rode to meet her. When he reined in he knew by her collar she had escaped from the Farm. A pleased smile crossed his face. The Farm paid a handsome reward for the return of escaped slaves.

The girl had sunk to the ground at his approach. She looked up at him piteously. He understood her need and gave her his wine-skin to wash out her parched mouth and drink her fill. Then he gave her a crust of bread, watched her devour it and gave her another. He eyed her calculatingly. She was not too weak to walk, he decided. He took a length cord from his pannier and bound her hands behind her. Then he tied a length of rope to her slave's collar. She made no effort to resist him and after holding the wine-flagon to her mouth for another long draught of strength-giving wine, he mounted his donkey. He tugged on the halter, waited for the slave to gain her feet and set off. He stopped frequently to allow the girl to rest whenever she fell, and two hours elapsed before he reached the farm he shared with his brothers. He was seen while he was still some distance from the farm and the family came out to meet them. It was a large family. He himself had five grown-up sons, with wives and children. His brothers had also fathered large families. All worked collectively in isolation, bearing crops to the distant town only every few months.

The family clustered around the slave, the women eyeing her curiously and the children timidly touching her. She was an awesome sight with long, tangled hair snagged with pine needles and twigs, the blood from her scratches dried black and her body coated with sweat-wet dust. They threw water over her until she was sluiced clean and led her into a barn. Straw was spread and her halter was tethered to a roof-beam, giving her enough slack to stretch out at ease. Bowls of water and food were placed beside her. Her hands were still bound behind her, but by kneeling she could lower her mouth to the bowls and eat and drink her fill. Then she was left alone.

She was tethered in the barn for many days, fed on houshold slops and the men of the farm took opportunity to visit her when they thought their wives were not watching. Then an elder son led her from the barn and mounted his donkey. She stumbled along behind him listlessly, so weary in mind and body she could not fear the future. At midday, when they sighted Brotan's Farm, the man stopped to eat, before the last, short, leg of their journey. When they were seen, guards opened the massive entrance doors and the man drove his heels into the donkey's flanks, trotting into the courtyard and dragging the girl behind him. 'I have come to claim the reward,' he shouted.

She arrived two hours after Surgeon Malem had been struck by another slave!

CHAPTER FIFTEEN

'This disobedience must be quelled!' sighed Brotan. But in the strange mood of dissatisfaction that had come upon him the disobedience of slaves no longer seemed important. 'We must impose stricter discipline.'

Surgeon Malem nodded gloomily. 'But . . . how?'

It was a problem to punish slaves. Confinement for days in a wooden box consumed their profitable labour. Flogging spoiled them for work and contract slaves had to be returned to their master without scars.

'First, the slaves who disrupted fertilisation. Shave their heads so the trouble-makers may be easily recognised,' ruled Brotan. This was a subtle punishment for females often causing them to weep. 'Ten days ceaseless labour without rest periods and only one handful of rice each day.' Brotan eyed Malem challengingly but the Surgeon nodded agreement. 'Stricter discipline for everybody,' decided Brotan. 'Legs and backs tingled often, and for little cause. A month of it will make them all respectful.'

'Agreed.' Malem fingered his bruised cheek. He didn't want a repetition of the offence.

'And special punishments for the slave who struck you and the one who escaped!'

Slave Number 122 was appalled that she'd struck a Master and expected a terrible flogging. But instead, she was ordered one stroke of the cane each day for seven days. Weaving stopped and the slave was ordered to bend over while everyone watched. The cane was whippy and the guard strong. He lashed and the girl screamed and danced in her agony. Those slaves who did not understand the punishment laughed at her comical capering. She was red-wealed but her skin was not broken. On the second day they did not laugh. The slave bent over with great reluctance and a new weal overlaid the first. The agonised prancing of the victim was watched in dread silence. On the third day the slave had to be ordered twice and had her calves tingled before she bent over. She whimpered all that night although her flesh was still not broken. On the next she had to be dragged out to receive her punishment. And on the fifth and sixth days two guards were needed to overwhelm her violent resistance to punishment. The seventh stroke was postponed for a fortnight on Surgeon Malem's orders. Angrily swollen flesh had blistered and he feared it would split open.

The slave who'd escaped was ordered one stroke of the cane every fourth day until her contract terminated. Iron shackles were placed upon her ankles joined by a short chain. Hobbling, she was put to the most unpleasant labours, cleaning sewage pipes, digging drainage pits and collecting garbage. After this, the other slaves laboured fearfully, giving no reason for fault-finding. Nevertheless, the guards tingled their backs and legs vigorously, as ordered, giving special attention to slaves with shorn heads.

But Brotan was still brooding and strangely discontent when a noble called who wished to buy a slave. He was returning from a journey far to the north and desired a young concubine. While young slaves were paraded before him, so that he could make his choice he affably answered Brotan's eager questions about Rome. They talked of the Games, of the theatre, of the new blocks of apartments being built and the fashions at Court. Brotan was absorbed by the conversation and his eyes glowed. It was five years since he'd visited the city and he had an over-whelming hunger for news of it.

The slaves on offer were pretty girls who had matured at twelve. They smiled with shy pleasure, as they'd been taught, when the noble's sensitive fingers explored their charms. But the noble shook his head. 'I want one who is younger. The more tender their years the more easily they learn.'

He was shown eleven-year olds with unformed breasts and found one to his liking. He stroked her hair and answered more of Brotan's questions.

'I long to see Rome,' sighed Brotan. 'I have grown stale in isolation.'

'Then join our caravan,' invited the noble. 'We are many and mounted. We have pack-mules and the journey will be swift.'

Abruptly Brotan knew his mood of discontent was because he wished to escape from the Farm. 'I'll join you!' he decided on the instant.

Surgeon Malem was troubled by the decision. 'And who will take charge?'

'You will,' said Brotan. 'You know my work and can do it.'

'Already my own work is more than I can handle,' grumbled Malem. But he reluctantly accepted Brotan's decision and when the caravan set off, Brotan rode with it.

CHAPTER SIXTEEN

Busy, bustling Rome revived all Brotan's nostalgic memories of the city. The depression that had overwhelmed him at the Farm dropped from him like a cloak. He needed money and went to his master's offices where a clerk looked up the accounts. Brotan had rarely needed money. For long years the Farm had supplied all his needs while he had steadily earned commission on the slaves and goods he had consigned to Rome. It amounted to a staggering sum and he was astonished to realise that if he wished he could buy a house and live in comfort for the rest of his days. He drew a small sum of money and, respecting his promise to Malem, visited the College of Surgeons where he learned a medical student had accepted a job as Malem's assistant. 'Tell him to be ready to leave within a few days,' said Brotan. 'He will ride back with me.'

Brotan happily explored the streets of Rome, relishing the noise and the smells, the bustling crowds and the colourful wares offered by stall-keepers. It was like drinking a vintage wine that warmed and sharpened his mind. He sought accommodation but Rome was over-crowded and he could find only modest lodgings. He strolled through the Park, joined a crowd listening to a heated debate between supporters of opposing charioteers and then made his way to the Baths where he watched the athletics, the ball-games and wrestling, the racing and the disc throwing. When the spectators drifted into the Baths, he went with them.

He was wearing a formal toga and was grateful to be free from its weight and discomfort. Nevertheless, when he entered the Sudatoria and dry heat wafted up through floor vents and enveloped him, he sweated profusely. He strolled up and down, eyeing the other bathers in the hope of seeing a familiar face. An attractive woman of thirty, accompanied by her slave, looked straight at him. For a moment he thought she had recognised him and smiled. She too smiled. But very coldly. She walked on without another glance at him. Brotan was fascinated. For long years he had known only downcast eyes and abject humility. It was an intriguing novelty to encounter a free woman who looked him straight in the eyes, and then turned away coldly, almost insultingly. He followed her. Not once did she turn around but when she passed through into the steamy Caldarium he was still behind her.

She reclined gracefully on a stone bench while her handmaiden massaged her flesh to help her sweat flow freely. Brotan sat opposite her, summoned a slave and had himself scraped with a strigil. 'My name is Brotan,' he told the woman.

Her eyes were cool and penetrating. 'I am Vanus,' she said boredly.

'I wish to know you better, Vanus.'

She smiled coldly. 'Why?' It was a disconcerting question.

'You fascinate me,' he said truthfully. 'Your attitude . . . excites me!'

'Indeed.' Her eyes looked down and stared fixedly. 'I would not have thought so,' she said with contempt in her voice.

Brotan was so accustomed to nudity it did not arouse him. Only when he thought erotically did he achieve an erection; and his interest in Vanus was for her aloofness and independence. She was the antithesis of a humble and submissive slave. But he was stung by her criticism of his manliness and said sharply. 'I am not a young and impetuous officer who calls out his troops at a mere rumour the enemy approaches. I conserve my forces until battle is joined.'

Her eyes were mocking. 'It might amuse me to subdue your

arrogance. But your belly is as disgustingly swollen as a pregnant woman's!'

He looked down at himself as the strigil scraped across his abdomen. It sank deep into soft and sweaty flesh and reamed out lines of dirt. 'For two days I have ridden a dusty road,' he excused himself.

'You are not of Rome?' She leaned back, her breasts firm and her stomach youthfully flat, unblemished by the marks of child-bearing.

'I was born in Rome,' he said and to his surprise heard himself adding. 'I may take up residence here and buy a small business to amuse myself.'

'What is your business, Brotan?'

'I manufacture cloth. But I have spent too many years at the trade and have grown weary of it. Perhaps now I should enjoy the many pleasures that Rome can offer.'

'To seek pleasure in Rome, a man needs money.'

'Money is no problem.'

'If only you were not *so fat*!' she sighed and he thrilled at the novelty of being criticised. 'You must sweat often and eat less,' she decided.

'I will, if you encourage me, Vanus.'

They left the steam room together, cooled down in the Tepidarium and then swam in the cold pool. Brotan dressed quickly but her face showed surprise when she found him awaiting her outside. She walked straight past him to her waiting litter. He followed her and when she would have entered her litter stepped forward quickly. 'Will you not invite me to your home,' he pleaded with unaccustomed humility.

Her eyes were cold. 'Am I to be one of your pleasures while you are in Rome?'

'I cannot deny you are beautiful. But my pleasure is in talking with you.'

She laughed mockingly. 'It is my mind and my tongue you adore, little fat man?'

He'd never been so insulted. He was a master, accustomed to respect. Yet strangely, her contempt and cold grey eyes fascinated him immeasurably. He was enjoying a strange satisfaction in being scorned. 'Will you not offer me a glass of wine?' he pleaded.

Her eyes studied him. 'If you wish.' She made room in the litter alongside her. 'My sandal fits badly,' she said as the litter swayed into movement. 'Remove it and mend it.'

He went down on one knee to remove her sandal. A cord needed to be re-tied. While he fitted the sandal on her foot, she raised her other foot and placed it lightly upon the back of his neck. 'Now I humble your arrogance, little fat one!' Her laughter wounded him. But he experienced a strange thrill at the reversal of the role which he had played so long. *She* was the master and *he* was her humble slave.

'May I arise, Mistress?' he asked, playacting.

She also playacted. 'No, slave!' The pressure of her foot upon his neck increased until he understood and lowered his lips to her foot, kissing her toes with a reverence that was not entirely pretended. He was deeply stirred by the huskiness in her voice when she said: '*Thus* must you be my slave.' She kept him kneeling until the litter bearers set them down outside her house.

Vanus's mother had been the concubine of a wealthy Patrician. She had been given her freedom, a modest dwelling and a comfortable income when she became pregnant. Vanus had been born free, had been well-educated and had discovered she was strangely attractive to some men. She'd had five husbands, all wealthy. Two were army officers killed on active service, two had sought a separation, and one had disappeared. When Vanus's mother died, the daughter inherited a comfortable residence, and already had an income that enabled her to live elegantly.

Brotan followed Vanus when she swept into the house, through the vestibule and into the salon. He was enjoying this adventure, thrilled by its contrast to what he had known for so many years. Vanus ignored him while her handmaiden removed her palla. She settled gracefully on a reclining couch wearing a short, doric tunic and gestured to a stool. 'Sit, Brotan!'

The stool was very low and uncomfortable. He arranged the folds of his toga and knew she watched him with mocking amusement. A handmaiden brought food and drink and then retired. 'You are arrogant, little fat slave,' said Vanus and her grey eyes were mischievous over the rim of her wine cup. 'You are accustomed to giving orders?' she asked shrewdly.

'Strict obedience is essential for efficient production.'

'You are an efficient manufacturer?'

'Yes.'

Her eyes challenged him. 'Why do you not order me?'

'You would not obey,' he said simply.

She laughed. 'But when I order, *you* obey?'

'Because . . . you fascinate me.'

'You surrender to my will, then, little fat slave?' Her eyes glowed. 'I am a woman of strange appetites. I consume and devour and am excited by power. You sense this in me. It thrills you to excite me!'

'That may be.' His mouth was dry.

'I dislike you, little fat slave. Go! Now! You anger me.'

His pride suffered but a strange compulsion kept him glued to his stool, his legs cramped while he sweated in the swathes of his toga.

'I will call slaves to throw you out,' she warned.

'Please,' he pleaded. 'Allow me to stay. To watch you, to listen to you.'

'Then do not breathe so heavily. You snort like a pig!'

Brotan held his breath. His face flushed and sweat rolled down his cheeks.

A handmaiden entered. 'It is Bachus, Mistress.'

'Show him in.'

Bachus was a strapping, fair-haired youth who eyed Vanus adoringly. 'I have counted the hours to be at your side, Vanus,' he greeted her. He gave Brotan a glance and then ignored him. 'Today you are even more beautiful.'

Vanus beckoned and Bachus joined her on the reclining couch where they talked intimately. His hands trembled with emotion and his eyes glowed. Presently he stood up, took her hands and drew her to her feet. She looked at Brotan without seeing him. 'You will go,' she stated. 'My lover will take me to my bed-chamber.'

'I wish to stay,' he pleaded.

'You will wait long.'

'I will wait,' he said humbly.

'You will go,' she ordered. 'Or you will remain seated there until I return.'

Brotan bowed his head in deference and wondered at himself. She humiliated him; ordered him to remain seated like a castigated slave; and yet, he found a strange pleasure in this game. As time passed he could have stood and stretched his cramped legs. But his pleasure would have been diminished if he'd cheated. His aching legs became numb and his toga wet with sweat, yet he extracted piquancy from his discomfort as though his endurance would win him a prize.

It was a long time before they returned. Vanus kissed the youth tenderly before a handmaiden showed him out. Then she saw Brotan. 'Why are you here! I told you to go!'

'I await you, Mistress,' he said humbly.

Her face was cold with displeasure. 'Then you will wait long, little fat man.' She ordered a handmaiden to prepare her bath and went away.

Was he mad? Brotan wondered. What would Surgeon Malem think of him? And how the Farm slaves would secretly ridicule him! Yet he was determined to prove something inexplicable. He remained seated while long hours dragged past, gaining an inner strength from his martyrdom.

Vanus eventually returned to the salon, wearing a cool chiton of gossamer material. She did not glance at him. She reclined on a couch and ordered food to be brought. Only after it was served did she acknowledge him. 'Why do you wait, little fat slave?'

'I wait for you, Mistress,' he said softly.

'Why?'

'To serve you, Mistress.'

Her grey eyes were cold. 'Stand up, slave.

He stood unsteadily, gritting his teeth against the pain of cramped muscles. On impulse he lowered his eyes as slaves had always lowered their eyes to him.

'A slave is not a master and cannot wear a toga,' she stated.

He removed his toga and stood before her submissively, his

nudity an added humiliation as her eyes probed his physical defects. 'Sweaty beast,' she said disgustedly. 'You smell. Your belly is loathsome, your legs too short and your chest flabby. You affront my sight.' She paused, then said bleakly. 'Approach, slave, and kneel.'

He kneeled before her and she gave him a cord of golden silk. 'Your halter, slave!'

He fastened it around his neck like a collar and gave her the free end. His fingers trembled.

'Feed me!'

He placed delicacies upon her tongue, wiped her lips with a napkin and held the wine cup while she drank. When she took half-chewed food from her mouth and threw it, as to a dog, he snapped at it eagerly. When she had eaten her fill she relaxed gracefully. 'Go now, she ordered. 'I will retire to my bedchamber'.

'I plead my Mistress to allow me to stay.' He hung his head.

'Do you wish to remain seated on a stool throughout the night, slave?'

'If it is my Mistress's wish,' he whispered.

'You will sleep on the floor at the foot of my bed,' she decided. She rose and led him by his halter to her bedchamber. Two handmaidens waited upon her but she sent them away. 'Disrobe me,' she ordered.

She relaxed languidly with closed eyes and a soft smile upon her lips while he brushed her hair. His arm was aching before she gestured him away. 'I am ready to retire, slave.'

He prepared the sleeping couch pillows and stood submissively while she stretched out upon it. She lay upon her back with her legs straight and her arms at her sides. Once again he admired the unblemished flesh of her flat belly. 'Bring my whip, slave,' she ordered.

It was on the dressing-table, a silver-hafted whip as rigid as a cane. She lightly placed its tip upon his cheek. 'Take your place at the foot of the bed, slave.'

He stood at the foot of the bed, staring down upon her shapely ankles and feet. 'I adore your toes, Mistress. I will adorn them with golden rings set with rubies.'

'Humble yourself, slave.'

He lowered his lips reverently to her toes and then, suddenly overwhelmed by a great wave of tenderness, kissed them passionately.

The tip of the whip came down lightly upon the back of his head with a gentle guiding pressure. He brushed his lips upwards over her ankle, his kisses tingling her sensitive skin and her updrawn leg encouraging his adulation. Her skin was velvet smooth and its fragrance intoxicating. In the hollow behind her knee a hint of saltiness on her flesh inflamed him madly. Her voice was a deep throb. 'That is the way, slave. That is the way it must be.'

Brotan visited the administrator of his master's estates.

'You will not alter your mind?' pleaded the man.

Brotan shook his head. 'No. I am done. Surgeon Malem can do my work. But you must persuade him to agree. He will soon have a new medical assistant so he will not be overworked.'

'Surgeon Malem is not a factory supervisor. We need time to replace you. Will you return to the Farm for a few months so that . . .'

'No!' said Brotan. His eyes glowed strangely. The Administrator wondered if Brotan was losing his senses.

'I will not leave Rome,' said Brotan more quietly. 'I have squandered my life in isolation. Now I will begin to live again!'

'For three months more we will pay you very handsomely.'

'No. I will not leave Rome.'

The Administrator prepared a message authorising Surgeon Malem to supervise the farm, and Brotan drew a large sum of money from his account. He made purchases at a number of shops before he went to Vanus's residence. She was out visiting but he went to her bedchamber, removed his toga and set out the purchases on her dressing table. There was a leather slave-collar, embroidered with silver studs and attached to it a slender chain of pure silver. There were also five gold rings set with gems that flashed fire. He had encircled Vanus's toes with a silken thread to measure their size.

Vanus returned accompanied by a woman friend. When handmaidens had removed their clothing and left the chamber, the two women embraced with great tenderness. Without looking at Brotan, Vanus asked. 'Did you pay the household accounts?'

'I did.'

'And my dressmaker?'

'It was long overdue. A large account.'

'You paid it?'

'It was my pleasure. It is also my pleasure to buy you presents.' Brotan gestured to the dressing table.

'You cannot buy my esteem with trinkets. I am an expensive woman of many desires.' She turned her companion so both women faced Brotan while they fondled each other. 'Look at that disgusting belly, Bella!'

Bella's lips curled. 'What an animal!'

'It is a man, darling,' said Vanus. 'Full of arrogance and convinced it is worthy. It even believes it can be attractive to women!'

Bella's eyes were contemptuous. 'So ugly. So . . . loathesome!'

'But is serves,' said Vanus. She paused, and then added; 'to pay bills and lavish presents upon us.'

Ripples of laughter filled the room.

'Shall I send it away, Bella?' asked Vanus.

'Can it serve at all?' Bella doubted.

'It is not without its uses.'

'Then show me.'

'My whip, slave!' ordered Vanus. She took it and narrowing her eyes catlike, laid it softly upon Brotan's cheek. A gentle pressure turned his head on one side. 'What ugliness!' she said disgustedly. 'The bones so large and the skin so rough.' She laid the whip upon the other cheek, turning his head to the other side. 'A nose so big and so red-veined!'

Bella fondled Vanus while her eyes scorned Brotan. The whip turned his face towards the women and its tip circled around the flabby pouches of his chest. 'Nauseating,' said Vanus. 'Flabby flesh.' The whip traced lower, exploring the fleshy crease of his abdomen. 'Repulsive!' The whip traced downward, rustling through hair to probe and display his manhood derisively.

Bella was breathless with laughter. 'It's so . . . ridiculous!'

'Men *are* ridiculous,' said Vanus. She turned away from Brotan and led Bella to the sleeping couch. They sank down upon it and embraced lovingly. Without looking at Brotan, Vanus ordered: 'Slave. To your post!'

Brotan stood humbly at the foot of the bed and stared down at the gracefully entwined ankles. Hot joy surged through him.

'Slave!' ordered Vanus. Her voice was deep-throated and husky.

Brotan lowered his lips to the enchantment of soft-skinned ankles, kissing greedily. The tip of the guiding whip rested very gently upon the back of his head.

CHAPTER SEVENTEEN

Alexander called upon Melanos. She received him wearing a chiton opened at the front through which her belly swelled.

'It is thoughtful of you to call upon me, Alexander,' she said mischievously. She'd anticipated his visit and its reason.

'You are well?' he asked awkwardly.

'Yes, Alexander. I am well.' Melanos' eyes danced. 'It is thoughtful of you to be concerned about my condition.'

'I am,' he said. His words seemed so inadequate he added, 'You have no pain?'

'Pain? Come closer, Alexander. Closer.' She took his reluctant hand and pressed it firmly upon her belly. 'There!' she said.

He wondered what was expected of him. 'It's very swollen,' he ventured.

'Do you not notice?' She wriggled and then he felt something pulsing under his hand.

'Is it kicking, Alexander? Is it?'

He jerked his hand away as though it had been seared. His eyes were glassy and he felt ridiculous. Melanos chuckled richly. 'Are you afraid of new life, Alexander?'

He sat on the couch keeping a discreet distance between them. 'Birth is a woman's affair,' he said gruffly. He'd never given thought to the mystery of life and to be abruptly confronted with it frightened him.

'Do not fear, Alexander,' she teased. 'I will not call upon you to be my midwife.'

He glowered. Melanos always made him feel stupid and her swollen belly embarrassed him. He would have excused himself quickly except he had yet to fulfil the purpose of his visit. He cleared his throat. 'There is a matter I would like to discuss.'

'There is, Alexander?' asked Melanos sweetly.

'A matter of a slave,' he said gruffly.

'How unusual, Alexander. You *rarely* concern yourself with slaves.'

He ignored the sugared shaft. 'It was a fine jest you played upon me the other night, Melanos!'

'But you did not laugh, Alexander,' she said solemnly.

He shrugged his shoulders. 'The victim of a jest does not always laugh at the time. But later he understands the joke.'

'I am pleased you can laugh when the joke is against you.'

He suppressed a scowl. 'The slave is comely,' he mentioned casually.

'Mertice?'

'The *slave*,' he said pointedly.

'And?'

'A household can be graced by comely slaves. I will pay a good price for this one, Melanos.'

Melanos gestured to a handmaiden. 'I will bring her here,' Melanos said before he could protest.

Mertice entered wearing a flowing gown of soft material that clung to her faithfully and Alexander's heart gave an unexpected leap of pleasure. He stared at her entrance, seeing she was even more beautiful than he remembered. Her face was serene and dignified and her blue eyes cool, yet with a hidden promise of affection. Her long hair flowed over her shoulders like silken sunlight. She settled on a reclining couch with a grace she'd been made to practice, and in obedience to Melanos' orders showed Alexander no slavish humility.

'Alexander wishes to buy a slave, Mertice,' said Melanos with appalling bluntness.

Alexander flushed violently.

'Is it not so, Alexander?' insisted Melanos.

'It is my wish,' he mumbled.

'Well? What do you offer?'

He shot a quick glance at Mertice. Her blue eyes were fastened intently upon his as though she was trying to warn him.

'Two hundred sesterces,' he offered.

Melanos laughed. 'Ridiculous!'

'Three hundred!'

'Alexander,' Melanos chided.

'Four hundred!' he said. He was being foolish but he did not care.

Melanos shook her head. 'No Alexander.'

He looked at Mertice. His eyes consumed her. He *had* to possess her. He was wealthy and did not care what he paid. 'Five hundred sesterces.' It was a mad price that none could refuse.

'If I say no, Alexander, will you offer more?'

He was furious. 'I came to you to talk business. Why do you quibble dishonestly?'

'You are anxious to buy *this* slave?'

'I am.'

'Why, Alexander?'

He looked away, tongue-tied.

'You want her for your bed-chamber, do you not, Alexander? You have the whim to possess her, and the sesterces to indulge your whim.'

'A slave is a slave,' he said. 'A master is to be obeyed.'

'And when you have possessed her and your whim withers, what then, Alexander? Will you remember our jest and the high price you have paid? Will you seek revenge? Have you already devised many little torments to punish without marring her beauty?'

He glared speechlessly. Melanos had the uncanny knack of knowing what was in his mind before he knew it himself. 'A comely slave will grace my household,' he blustered.

'For five hundred sesterces you can have the pick of all beautiful slaves, Alexander.'

Alexander pointed at Mertice. 'I want *this* slave,' he said petulantly. '*This* one!'

'Mertice is not merely a slave,' said Melanos gently. 'She is also a companion. She has my complete trust. She is hostess in my stead while I am indisposed.'

'Then I will take her as a slave companion!' said Alexander angrily. 'I will pay a thousand sesterces! Why do you thwart me?'

'You wish her for *your* companion?' doubted Melanos. 'To have her at your side at all times, to escort her to spectacles, provide her with a bed-chamber and handmaidens, and let her rule over your household?'

He stared at Melanos as if she was mad. 'I do not wish a wife. What is a slave companion but a woman who must obey!'

'Mertice is my companion, and I have great need of her,' decided Melanos firmly. 'What need have you of a companion, Alexander?'

Frustration was an ache within him. He looked at Mertice with hopeless longing. 'I need to look upon her loveliness and have her at my side when it is my wish.'

'Then there is no problem, Alexander,' Melanos said softly. 'I am not selfish. Mertice will be free when you wish her to be your companion.'

His eyes glowed. 'That is generous, Melanos. I am grateful.'

'She will not enter your household,' Melanos stipulated.

Alexander stared. 'Why not?'

'The subtleties of your bedchamber are too exotic for a slave companion. Mertice will go abroad with you accompanied by handmaidens.'

'And where would we go?' demanded Alexander.

'You may walk together in the park. You will find Mertice a pleasing companion!'

Alexander jumped to his feet. 'Walk in the park!' he stormed. 'This is one jest too many, Melanos. Never again will you mock me. I too will have my jest and you also will writhe under the lash of ridicule!' He stormed away.

Melanos looked at her handmaidens in mock bewilderment. 'I wonder why he is angry?' she asked and the girls laughed with her. But when Melanos looked at Mertice her brow crinkled in annoyance. 'Stupid girl!' she scolded. 'Why do you cry? Have you not the wit to see him for what he is – a fool?'

Mertice nodded, but her shoulders shook. The tears were wet upon her cheeks.

Two riders rode out through the city gates and heeled their mounts into a canter. One was the escort guard who had accompanied Brotan to Rome and the other was Marcus, mounted upon Brotan's own horse. He glanced over his shoulder as the city gates retreated behind them, hoping wildly he might see Una beckoning for him to return. But it was a dream too mad to be realised. She had broken with him with finality. Swallowing the lump in his throat, Marcus looked ahead, thrusting Una out of his thoughts and concentrating upon his future.

'Slacken rein, Master,' suggested the guard. 'We must not tire our horses too quickly.'

'Two days you say?'

'If we ride long into the night and set off again before dawn.'

'It is hard riding?'

'There are mountains to cross.' The guard was uneasy. 'It is dangerous,' he added significantly.

'Dangerous? How?'

'Robbers lie in ambush. They will slit throats for fine clothes and a horse. We are two; they may be many.'

'Why then do we not wait to travel in caravan?'

'That is what I wished.' The guard glowered. 'But I have an urgent message. A caravan will not be ready for another week and will take seven days upon its journey.'

'What is the urgent message?'

The guard tapped his saddlebag. 'An authority for Surgeon Malem to supervise the Farm. Brotan has gone mad. A woman has turned his head and he will not leave Rome.'

'The Farm breeds healthy slaves?' asked Marcus with quickening interest.

The guard threw back his shoulders and sat proudly in his saddle. 'I am a Farm-bred slave,' he boasted.

'And with you at my side I have little fear of robbers,' said Marcus.

'I am an intelligent man, yet a cunning man,' said Diocles with a modest smile. 'I am honest in business but never allow my right hand to know what my left hand does. I am expert in some things and capable in most others. But when I must cope with my wife, I throw up my hands in despair!' He smiled comically at Hadrian who reclined opposite him. 'You do not have such difficulties, Hadrian?'

Hadrian smiled thinly, selected a peach from the fruit dish, and bit into it.

'Which is fortunate,' continued Diocles blandly. 'Because thus you can help me shoulder my burden.' He chuckled when Hadrian stiffened. 'Try a fig,' he encouraged. 'They're delicious.'

Diocles chewed a black grape, spat out its skin and pips and flourished a chubby hand. 'I am industrious. I dedicate myself to business. Litirus is a good and useful associate, Hadrian. Through him we prosper.' He chose another grape, chewed and spat. 'Poppea serves us too, wheedling and advising her husband.' Diocles smiled fondly. 'She is an animated little kitten. Now she has rejoined social life she is full of a zest for living. She wishes me to take her everywhere, see everybody, do everything. She burns the candle at both ends.' He paused and frowned. 'My candle too,' he said gloomily. 'Yet her enchanting vitality is inspiring and I do not complain.'

Hadrian listened expressionlessly.

'Valle understands the importance of our business relationship with Litirus,' commented Diocles. He chose a fig and cut its green skin with his thumbnail, peeling it open and sucking its juicy, red pulp into his mouth. He licked his sticky fingers. 'Wives are unpredictable,' he complained. 'Valle complains she is neglected. She protests she never goes anywhere nor sees anybody. She does not begrudge the time I spend with Poppea. She does not bite the hand that feeds her. But every day she complains more bitterly.' Diocles chubby face was comically wry as he spread despairing hands. 'She complains so long and so loud my poor head aches. It is a problem, is it not, Hadrian?'

'It is the nature of wives to be a problem,' agreed Hadrian tonelessly.

'But the ingenuity of men solve problems,' said Diocles. His eyes shone as though he had scored a major debating point. He reached for an apple and munched. 'Well?' he asked after some moments of silence. 'What are your suggestions?'

'Visit Barba the slaver,' said Hadrian spitefully. 'Buy Valle a slave escort like Strabo. Clothing him and parading him will distract her.'

'An uninspired suggestion!' said Diocles. 'One I have tried without success. Valle has three escort slaves, all magnificently costumed. When she goes abroad she is a spectacle that turns other women green with envy. But Valle is too mature to commit the indiscretions of Poppea. She has great esteem for social prestige. She would never allow a slave a favour, nor commit a social blunder.'

Hadrian stared down at his hands.

'Valle yearns for the company of a man upon whom she can lavish her warm friendship and affection.'

'Her search should not be unrewarding,' said Hadrian bleakly. 'She is a woman of great poise and charm.'

'But no longer young, Hadrian,' said Diocles gently. 'A mature woman has much to offer a man. But sagging, wrinkled flesh is a barrier only an understanding man will ignore.' He crinkled his brow in comic imitation of a wise man making a solemn judgement. 'Valle's qualities cannot easily be recognised. She needs an admirer who will combine financial politics with companionable affection.'

Hadrian's face was like stone.

Diocles sighed at his lack of co-operation. 'Valle has great affection for you, Hadrian. You always head our dinner invitations and when we talk of profitable business she always mentions your name. While I devote time to Poppea and promote our mutual interests, Hadrian, you are constantly in Valle's thoughts.'

Hadrian scowled. 'If it is Valle's wish, I will escort her to the theatre and other entertainments.'

Diocles smiled with satisfaction. 'For long it has been Valle's cherished dream to visit Trebula.' Diocles' eyes twinkled. 'Who better to escort her than its architect who is realising his own dream?'

Hadrian's face turned dark.

'You plan to go to Trebula next week, do you not, Hadrian?' said Diocles as though all was now arranged. 'Valle will be very happy. Make it a long visit, Hadrian. At least ten days. Valle will wish to inspect Trebula very leisurely.'

Hadrian's bath was ready when he arrived home and while he relaxed in the scented water Haesel kneeled beside him, massaging and cleansing the dust and sweat of the day from the pores of his skin. He was silent and bad-tempered and she did not talk, respecting his mood. But presently he said with resolution. 'Haesel. We will leave Rome and go far away. We will start a new life; the two of us. Alone.'

'But your work, Hadrian? Your business?'

'I have savings. We will not be wealthy. But neither will we be poor.'

'And Trebula? Who will finish building it?' She sensed the hurt within him.

But he was resolute. 'A dream can die,' he said. He looked at her and smiled sadly. 'So that another dream can live, Haesel.'

'What you propose is madness, Hadrian. Trebula is where we will live, together.'

'I do not wish our dream to be violated.'

'And who will violate it?' she asked softly.

He scowled. 'Diocles. And Valle. I am to escort her to Trebula and be her constant companion.'

'If you do not wish it and refuse, what then?'

'It is better we depart before Diocles is angered. He will renounce me as architect, cancel our business contracts and willingly lose a small fortune to impoverish me. He is a good friend but ruthless to those he believes betray him.'

'And you would give up everything to avoid Valle?'

He looked at her tenderly. 'Trebula is ours. Nobody will invade it.'

'Will you give up what is ours so recklessly, Hadrian? Valle can come and go. But Trebula will still remain ours!'

'You do not understand, little one. Valle would never leave my side. She would be with me everywhere, at all times. While you would be my slave, bound to serve me, never for a moment would I be able to look into your eyes or hold your hand.'

'We would be unhappy only for a short time, Hadrian. Afterwards, we will have our happiness again.'

'You could bear it?' he asked disbelievingly.

She smiled but her eyes were misty. 'I am a very understanding slave, Hadrian.'

'The woman is an octopus, Haesel; greedy and consuming. I will be swallowed whole, digested and excreted.'

Haesel laughed through her tears. 'Do not anger Diocles. Take Valle to Trebula. If our dream is of value, Hadrian, we must pay a price for it.'

CHAPTER EIGHTEEN

Surgeon Malem made his first round of the day and stood watching the deft movement of slaves at their weaving. He'd always ignored mechanical processes as inferior to anatomical reproduction. But now circumstances compelled him to pay it attention, he was fascinated by its precision. He inspected a recently made roll of cloth and had already learned enough of weaving to judge it to be well made. The stricter discipline was achieving good results and work was maintaining a consistently high standard. A slave he remembered sending for fertilisation a short time ago stooped over, diligently weaving coloured thread into a pattern. Out of habit he cupped her breast and squeezed it, seeking evidence of conception. But he had much to do and soon passed on to watch slaves building an additional storehouse. There was no limit to the land that could be built upon and with sudden enthusiasm he issued new instructions. They would begin to build yet another storehouse. It would be high and airy and with many windows to give good light. It would have many cupboards and a long writing table. It would house all his breeding records so they could be referred to easily. If a slave with the ability could be found, she would be made an assistant to his records clerk.

A guard brought him his horse and they rode out to inspect the fields. One field was being broken up. The sun had baked all moisture from it and the ground was like stone. A long line of slaves stooped and hammered at the earth with short, pointed stakes, breaking it up into a shallow furrow. It was back-breaking labour, slow, and yielding small reward for the energy expended. Surgeon Malem's brow furrowed thoughtfully and he turned to the guard. 'Have you tried other ways to break the land?'

'This is the way it is always done, Sire.'

'It is slow.'

The guard shrugged his shoulders. 'It is work for slaves, Sire.'

'You will try another way,' decided the Surgeon. 'You will drive a stake into the ground at an angle. Then a rope will be passed around the stake and hauled upon by many slaves. The stake will then cut a furrow. Give me your sword and I will show you.' Malem demonstrated with the swordpoint, showed that when drawn across the ground it ploughed a furrow.

'The wood is soft and the ground is hard, Sire,' the guard objected.

'Then use an iron stake,' decided Surgeon Malem. His quick mind already visualised what was required. 'Make it this way.' He traced a design on the ground with the swordpoint. 'The iron will shape to a point, thus. A ring for the hauling rope will be here. And here, the iron will curve outwards so that as the point drives deep, the loose earth will be guided away from the furrow.'

Surgeon Malem rode on. His mind seethed with new ideas to improve the Farm. He felt vaguely guilty that he had neglected his medical work but his new assistant was capable and learned quickly.

Marcus had been startled by the enormous number of patients he had to attend upon. But Surgeon Malem had explained his examination routine, which brought order to what at first seemed chaos. A diligent clerk kept good records and the overseers had the patients due for examination lined up ready for him.

Marcus found the work exciting because new horizons of medical knowledge were being opened up. It delighted him to learn that flesh and blood could be so easily moulded to the Farm's needs. Surgeon Malem's development of wet-nurses was a thrilling surprise. He had known some mothers prolonged the suckling of their infants. But he had never suspected that suckling could be deliberately prolonged for years. Yet the process was quite logical. The feeding-women were segregated and sat on the straw in compulsory inactivity to conserve their strength while their bodies manufactured life-giving milk. They were fed an abundance of nourishing food, boiled rice, bread, fruit and meat soup. The feeders' bodies adapted to the system. Their hips, buttocks, bellies and thighs stored fat until, although young, even rising to their feet was an effort that made them wheeze. Marcus knew that even small-breasted mothers can give more milk than their infants need. But all the feeders became big-breasted. Prolonged suckling opened up the milk-ducts until milk flowed abundantly and the breasts enlarged into milk storehouses. Most feeders could suckle several infants at one feeding.

Although excited by this biological discovery Marcus was uneasy about the feeders' personal feelings as human beings; until he studied them. They sprawled contentedly in the straw, lazy-eyed and grossly fat. But their faces were serene and when they changed their position they held enormous breasts with tender protectiveness so they would not swing. They were sleek and smug and totally and happily absorbed in themselves as they cared for their nipples. They were immensely proud when feeding time approached and milk flowed easily at the slightest coaxing of their fingers.

The breeders also surprised Marcus. Romans did not have large families and two or three children do not spoil a woman's figure. But most breeders had produced fifteen or more infants and the ravages of childbirth had given them wrinkled bellies with over-stretched flesh that hung in limp folds. He wondered if the slaves resented being transformed into functional machines. But the breeders were as placidly contented as a herd of cows. One young slave bearing a second infant had been indicated by Surgeon Malem as a possible breeder. She'd had her head shaved and her haunches were sore from a recent caning. No slave spoke direct to a master but he'd asked her through the overseer if she was content to become a breeder. She'd answered tonelessly: 'What else can I do?'

There was too much brutality. An infant cried and a pregnant mother with a shaved head instantly sprang forward to comfort it. Nevertheless, a guard swung his whip, red-wealing her calves to speed her. The guards used their whips too freely, Marcus observed. Few slaves survived the day without having their legs or backs tingled. He spoke to a guard about it.

'Surgeon Malem's orders, Sire.'

Marcus resolved to take it up with Surgeon Malem. While inspecting the latrine he found another cause for complaint. The cleaner was a slave on a punishment diet and long labour hours. Her body was hard and muscular but without an ounce of fat. Her ankles were shackled until she could only hobble, and being denied tools she was compelled to scoop up sewage with her hands to fill the bucket to cart it away. 'Why is this?' Marcus demanded.

'It is punishment, Sire,' said the guard. 'Well deserved. She escaped.'

'There are other less unhealthy punishments.'

The guard shrugged his shoulders. 'Surgeon Malem's orders, Sire.'

In the weaving factory Marcus grappled with the new problem that Surgeon Malem had dropped into his lap. He examined a slave who'd been sent to the guards for insemination. This three-monthly check showed she had not conceived. But the records clerk sweated with concentration as he tried to decide how the new system should now be applied. With his mania for precise records, Surgeon Malem had introduced an insemination check. All the twenty or more stud guards noted down every day the collar numbers of the slaves they'd served. After the system's first day, by cross-checking, Surgeon Malem had learned that some slaves had been served only once or twice, whereas others had been served three or four times. In a week, some slaves had received only seven inseminations, as against twenty or thirty. With twelve or fifteen slaves awaiting service, some being called away at feeding time, it was difficult to ensure a strict rotation. Slaves could change their position in the queue and the guards, being human, might have preferences. But Surgeon Malem's new system was based upon quantity of inseminations combined with variety of donors. In future, only four slaves would report on an appointed day for insemination. They would be served in strict rotation, ensuring a variety of donors. After a lapse of ten days the four slaves would attend again for a second insemination. And ten days later for a third. By this method full advantage could also be taken of the female fertility cycle. Marcus thought the system was too concentrated. But Surgeon Malem overruled him. If new methods were not tried it could not be known if they could succeed, he'd argued.

But the clerk and Marcus had to put this new system into practice, changing the records from fifteen slaves being serviced throughout a week, to four slaves being served every tenth day. The two wrestled with the records and decided that this slave, and three others of her category, should report to the guards in nine days' time. And at this moment a guard came hurrying for Marcus. He was needed urgently.

The slave lay pain-wracked, her body running with sweat. As Marcus approached her eyes rolled up and she gave a keening scream that tore through her. She was young and it was her first child. Marcus examined her swiftly before the next pain racked her. He stood at the foot of the bed. 'Take these away,' he ordered, pointing at the wooden boards upon which the slave's feet rested. 'Give her the straining ropes,' he said. He waited until another wave of pain gathered its strength, then raised the girl's feet and braced them against his shoulders. He leaned forward as she bore down with a muscular spasm. 'Strain,' he urged. 'Strain!'

Melanos sobbed. Sweat was wiped from her brow. The veins of her outflung arms stood out like whipcord and her fingernails gouged deep into her palms. The pain swelled up again, bigger and more tearing than she could bear. Yet despite her agony, her muscles strained to their utmost. Blackness swooped down upon her and then with a pulsing rush came immense and sweet relief.

She lay panting, exultation dissolving her weakness. She would have raised her head but a gentle hand restrained her. A comforting voice soothed: 'Not yet. Not yet.'

She waited, tormented by anxiety until she heard the baby cry.

'It is done, Mistress,' said Mertice.

'No . . . imperfections?' whispered Melanos.

'None, Mistress. She's beautiful and adorable; she has her mother's eyes!'